MINE

A NOVELLA

Fiona Quinn

Publisher's Note: This is a work of fiction. Names, characters, places, and incidents are a product of the author's imagination. Locales and public names are sometimes used for atmospheric purposes. Any resemblance to actual people, living or dead, or to businesses, companies, events, institutions, or locales is completely coincidental.

Cover Design by Melody Simmons from eBookindiecovers

Author portrait by Donna Toone from Studio M

Font used with permission from Microsoft

Ordering Information:

Quantity sales. Special discounts are available on quantity purchases by corporations, associations, and others. For details, contact the "Special Sales Department" at the email address above.Mine/ Fiona Quinn. -- 1st ed.

For: Jamie, Scott, Teresa, Diane, Hildie, and Tawny – it was very Unlucky that I got to know you.

For new release notifications, free offers, gifts, and sneak peeks for members only, please sign up for Fiona Quinn's mailing list. I don't want to leave you out of the fun!

The **newsletter sign** up is: http://goo.gl/97x0QX

ONE

....

Kate Hamilton stared down at her Uncle Owen's face in the casket, barely able to recognize him. Somehow, the funeral director had molded and painted her uncle's features into a pleasant, peaceful expression. There had never been anything pleasant or peaceful about the man in life. Everyone in Scarborough would agree that Owen Jenkins was one of the most cantankerous and disagreeable people that God had ever created.

Her aunt, Emma Jenkins, told stories about how Uncle Owen hadn't always been that way. She had said that before he left for Vietnam, he was charming and gentle-hearted. No one but Aunt Emma could remember that far back in his history. Over the last fifty years, all his meanness had robbed the town of the happier memories of him. Uncle Owen had been the official town curmudgeon.

And now, no one cared that he was dead.

"I'm not expecting anyone to stop by tonight." Aunt Emma turned a page of her library book.

"What about from the church?" Kate asked.

Aunt Emma didn't look up as she spoke. "Not for paying their last respects. I imagine they'll come to the funeral tomorrow.

The paper said I hired Maggie May's for the catering. People will want to get out of the house, get something free to eat, and gossip. I don't expect a crowd, but it won't be empty neither."

"Surely, your friends will be there to support you."

"Perhaps a few. I pushed the funeral up a day, or I'd have no hope of anyone coming at all."

"Why's that?" Kate asked.

Aunt Emma put her finger where she left off reading. "There's a pig-picking Saturday afternoon with music and politicians, and what-all. The whole town will turn out. Perhaps I'll go, too. Rose said they'll have a soft-serve ice cream truck."

Kate moved to the chair next to her aunt and sat down, yanking the short skirt of her black dress to its full length, as she aimed for modesty. The call telling Kate that Uncle Owen had died had come just as she loaded her last suitcase into the back of her Ford Explorer. She had dashed back into the house and grabbed something black to wear, only to realize later that her dresses ran more along the lines of cocktail party than proper mourning attire. She saved the plainer of the two for the funeral. Aunt Emma lent her a cardigan to help hide the dress's low neckline.

True to her aunt's word, no one showed up for the viewing. An hour had passed, and they had another one yet to go. Kate wished her aunt had warned her earlier, or she had the foresight to bring a book, too.

Kate stared into the forest scene of one of the oil paintings decorating the small room, rubbing her thumb over the Celtic design on the ring adorning her index finger. Her mind wandered back to what had happened on Tuesday, and the awkwardness of her good-bye as she left her husband. His decision, not hers.

"I need you to leave, for your own damned good," Ryan had argued.

It had killed Kate to drive away. It was her place—no, her *right* to be by his side, supporting him. But he had said to go, and she was afraid of what he might do if she didn't comply. Thank goodness the school year at John Adams High had wrapped up, and she'd already handed in her students' final science grades. Thank goodness Aunt Emma had welcomed her with open arms. And of course, she owed a big thanks to Tim. Just as his image bubbled up in her mind, Kate turned around to see Detective Tim Gibbons walking toward her and Aunt Emma.

Aunt Emma was on her feet, opening her hands to welcome him. "How kind of you to stop by tonight," she said.

"How are you holding up, Mrs. Jenkins?"

"Kate's here," Aunt Emma gestured in her direction. "She's such a blessing. I was so glad when she decided to visit for the summer. And then this happened." Aunt Emma fingered her cross-pendant. "I can't say this will make her stay any worse, though. I expect it might improve it considerable with Owen gone."

Tim nodded, "He was a hard man to like, but you stayed with him—it speaks of the depth of your love."

Shame and resentment filled Kate. As horrible as Uncle Owen had been, he never threw her aunt out.

Aunt Emma reached out and grasped Tim's forearm; her serenity crumbled. "Some men, they lost their legs or their sight in the war. Owen lost his goodness. He came out of the war crippled and broken. His ugliness was not his fault."

Kate rubbed her hand over her aunt's back, her gaze fastened on Tim.

Tim was taller than he had been in high school. The laugh lines that crinkled the corners of his eyes when they were younger now permanently etched his tanned skin. The fifteen years that she had lived in Boston hadn't changed him much. He looked good. This was trouble, and Kate knew it as sure as she knew that the next thing he'd say would be…

"Look at you, Katydid."

"Not much to see." She dragged a smile into place and pulled the cardigan tighter around her body.

"Boston agrees with you."

4

"It does indeed." Kate nodded.

"Well, welcome home. Glad to have your help at the police station. Though it's not much of a place to do a CSI internship. You're going to end up bored." He stuck his hands in his pockets. "We still roll up the sidewalks come dark."

"Good. I could use a little boredom." As soon as the words popped out of her mouth, Kate regretted them. Her troubles weren't meant for public consumption.

Tim's gaze locked on hers. He seemed to reach right in and pry her secrets loose. As the lead detective on the small town police force, Kate imagined Detective Tim Gibbons had honed his dowsing skills—sharpened his people-reading acuity. It was a skill Kate loved about him. One of the many things she'd loved about him. But now it felt invasive, and she took a step back.

"Where's Pam?" Aunt Emma asked.

Tim pulled his wallet from his back pocket. "She's home with the boys tonight. Billy has a fever from his new tooth." He grinned at the picture of his family he held out for them to see.

"Oh, they're beautiful, Tim," Aunt Emma gushed. "Your eldest is getting so big, and looks the spitting image of his daddy."

A movement from the doorway caught Kate's attention. "Good evening," she said to the man standing there.

Aunt Emma glanced around. "Doctor Javarti, thank you for coming. Let me introduce you to my niece."

Tim gave Aunt Emma a light kiss on her cheek. "I'm on duty. I need to head on now. Kate." He nodded in acknowledgement, shook hands with the new man, and left.

"Kate, I'd like you to meet the physician who tried to save your Uncle Owen, Dr. Omid Javarti."

"My condolences," he said to Kate, then focused his attention on Aunt Emma. "I'm very sorry for your loss, Mrs. Jenkins. But your husband has found peace. After so many years of torment, he's at rest."

Kate detected the smallest accent in Omid's English. The way he stood and the European cut of his suit—which she was much more likely to see in her adopted home of Boston than in southwest Virginia—made Kate wonder how this cosmopolitan man had found his way to Scarborough.

"That's very kind," Aunt Emma said. "Owen just wouldn't listen to good reason. Never would follow his doctor's orders. We both knew he was risking a heart attack."

To Kate's surprise, her aunt pulled a handkerchief from her sleeve and dabbed her eyes. Had Kate been married to someone like Owen, she would be celebrating. Upon hearing the news, Kate's first thought was that Uncle Owen dying of a heart attack was irony at its best. Most folks swore the man was heartless.

"Even so, a sudden loss can shock the system," Dr. Javarti said. "Please tell me if you need anything in the next days or weeks—something to help you sleep, or to deal with any anxiety or depression." He and Aunt Emma walked to the casket. Aunt Emma touched the handkerchief to her eyes, and Kate realized her aunt was crying. Kate was ashamed of her flippancy. She knew better.

⚜ ⚜ ⚜

Even with the funeral planned for early morning, the bright rays of sunshine hammered Kate's head. Her silk dress clung to her thighs as the humidity rose. Aunt Emma and Kate were the only ones in black. Most dressed for a garden party, though Kate noticed, a few people wore shorts as if Uncle Owen's funeral was their first stop on errands day, and they'd be heading over to the Quick-Pick Groceries after the service. The guests smiled and gossiped. There wasn't a sad face amongst them.

Kate had to take her aunt's sweater off when they left the air-conditioned comfort of the sanctuary. There she stood, dressed as if for a Friday night martini with the girls, listening to the preacher chanting from the Book of Common Prayer, "Ashes to ashes, dust to dust…"

Kate glanced over her shoulder in time to receive Doris Arthur's wilting stare.

"Stay away from Doris if you can help it," her aunt whispered in her ear. "If those looks were daggers, you'd keel over dead and share the grave with your uncle."

"Why? What did I ever do to her?"

"Let's talk about it when we get home. We don't need the gossips revved up, and Sally Jo can read lips." Aunt Emma reached out and took Kate's hand.

After Aunt Emma placed the first shovelful of dirt over the coffin, the finality of Owen's death hit Kate. Not that she'd miss him, but what about her aunt? Would she be okay?

Shortly after, they all headed back to the assembly room for refreshments. A buzz from her phone stopped Kate's progress. After a quick peek at the screen, she halted. "Aunt Emma, I'll be there in a minute. I'm going to the garden to take this call."

Kate emerged from under the tree, cell phone still in her hand. She bent and used the hem of her dress to wipe away the last of her tears. When she stood up, she found Tim standing in front of her, his hands resting lightly on his hips. He took in her appearance, but refrained from comment until they reached the church.

"Why don't you slide in here? It goes to Reverend Pine's office, and he has a bathroom. You might want a minute to yourself to freshen up." He pushed the door open, but didn't follow her.

One glance in the mirror told Kate why he had shepherded her away. Red splotches ringed her eyes, her mascara ran to her chin, her hair was a mess of humid curls, and sticktights covered her fanny. She was a wreck—inside and out. She pulled herself together as best she could. When she emerged from the bathroom, she held her head high as she headed back out the side door to find Tim, leaning against the brick with his hands shoved in his pockets.

He swept his gaze over her. "You'll be okay. People will chalk it up to grief, though they'll wonder why." He pushed off the wall. "I came by to get you because I'm heading over to a crime scene, and I'd appreciate your help. You're not supposed to start 'til Monday. You can say no."

"No problem. I'm happy to help. I need to check on my aunt, and then…should I follow you?"

"Let's leave your Explorer with Mrs. Jenkins. I've got the squad car. They're bringing in the forensics van now, so you'll have supplies. Officer Mandrel, who has the most experience with CSI, is on his honeymoon." Tim moved towards his car as Kate climbed the granite stairs.

Back in the assembly hall, she grabbed a plastic cup of ice-cold lemonade, and chugged it down in one gulp. Most everyone had left. There were a few ladies dawdling over the ham biscuit tray. Doris was one of them. She glared at Kate, clearly vexed about something, her toe tapping and her hands resting on her hips

Kate sent the woman a bewildered glance, then found her aunt and explained Tim's request. "Would you be okay if I leave?"

"It's fine, dear. Rose is going home with me, so I'll have company."

After handing her aunt the car keys, Kate kissed her cheek and said, "Wish me luck."

The heat of the day wrapped itself around Kate as she pushed through the heavy wooden doors. She had forgotten the extremes of southern temperatures. Outside, it was a screen door away from hell; inside, it was iceberg-cold with multiple air units cranked to their highest settings. *Butter in a skillet,* Kate mused as she tiptoed across the graveled parking lot to keep her high heels from sinking into the stones. Thankfully, Tim had the engine running in the car, and the interior was plenty cool as she slid in. Hot then cold, hot then cold— as a child it hadn't fazed her, but she'd lost her acclimatizing skills, and the sudden shifts left Kate nauseated.

"You okay?" Tim asked.

"Is there time for us to run by my house so I can get changed?"

Tim glanced at her shoes. "We'll have to. You can't go into a crime scene in heels, you're bound to fall over and destroy evidence." He sent her a smile, but the corners of his mouth remained grim.

Kate's scalp itched with apprehension.

"You've got to make it quick. As soon as hazmat gives us the all-clear, we need to be ready to go."

"Hazmat?" Kate's voice squeaked.

"Just a precaution."

They drove through town toward the river. As he pulled onto the highway, Tim said, "I'm assuming those tears weren't for your uncle."

"No." She brushed at imaginary lint on her skirt. "I can't say I'm sorry Uncle Owen's gone."

Tim reached over the seat, produced a bottle of water, and handed it to Kate.

"How's everything in Boston?"

She rolled the bottle across her forehead and the back of her neck before taking a swig. "I'll tell you what, how about you brief me on the crime scene instead?"

11

TWO

....

Kate stood at the rear of the CSI van, gathering camera equipment. Dressed in a Tyvek suit, she carried a pair of booties with her as she walked to the front door. On the way, Kate passed a woman sitting under the oak with her legs spread out in front of her, her face drooped, and her eyes looked vacant. An EMT hovered nearby.

"This is Kate Hamilton, she'll be assisting today," Tim announced, as he pulled his shoe coverings over his boots and signed himself in with the officer guarding the crime scene taped entry. Kate followed suit.

Standing in the foyer, Kate's breath clouded in front of her.

"We have to get the temperature down on days like this, so we have time to work," Tim said as he organized the equipment.

"No medical examiner?" Kate asked.

"We're too far away. We do their tests, and send the information on with the bodies. They have a contract with the funeral home to provide transport. I'll give them a call when we wrap up."

Kate's teeth chattered, and she hugged her arms around herself. She was glad she had an excuse for her reaction, and that Tim would assume she was cold and not lily-livered. She didn't want a bad reputation for being an emotional wreck before she even started her internship.

She and Tim stood in the archway separating the hall from the family room, observing the scene. Two teens lay dead, crumpled like discarded papers on the floor.

One boy lay near the sofa. He wore a pair of basketball shorts and a T-shirt. His legs were thin, and he was barefooted. The beginnings of an adolescent mustache trimmed an otherwise baby face surrounded by a cloud of blond curls. His complexion was gray, and Kate wanted nothing more than to rush in and wrap him in a warm blanket, to rub circulation back into his skin, and for him to wake up and say…anything at all.

The second boy lay near the TV. Like his friend, he was dressed for a hot summer day. He lay on his back, with his arms and legs sticking up at odd, implausible angles. Kate realized this teen had been moved since rigor had set in. *The EMTs must have turned his body over to check for vital signs.* His position made it look like he was flailing, trying to get up off his back. He had the same waxy look as the mannequins Kate's forensics class had practiced on.

There weren't as many flies as she had anticipated, probably one of the reasons they cranked the air conditioning up. The TV was off. There were no obvious signs of trauma. The room was neat as a pin.

Kate opened her mouth to speak; she had to stop and clear her throat before trying again. "This place was checked out for carbon monoxide?"

"Hazmat green-lighted our being in here. That's the mom outside," Tim said. "She came home and found this." He pointed toward the dark-haired boy near the TV. "She turned her son over and tried to revive him while the paramedics were on their way, but the kids had been dead for hours. The EMTs realized the bodies were in rigor. They moved her outside, cranked the air conditioning, and handed the scene over to us. We'll start by taking pictures." Tim gestured towards the black cases.

Kate stared at the boys' bodies. "These are children." Her words were barely audible.

"Kate, get the camera." Tim gripped her arms and spun her toward the equipment. "Your first scene is the hardest. You told me you had done an autopsy."

"I have," Kate's teeth chattered. "But it was a very old man." She leaned down to unzip the case. "I imagined he had lived a full and happy life." She looked back over her shoulder at the family room. "These are high schoolers. They should be…"

"Alive. I know. But we have a job to do." Tim's tone was steady and calm. "The family will need to understand what happened here. It's the only thing we can do for them that'll make any difference. Focus on doing the very best job you can. You're a scientist. You're a professional."

Those were the words Kate needed to hear to spur her into action. She followed Tim's directives, as she desperately swiped at her imagination as it overlay a macabre slide show of her own students' faces onto the corpses'. Short, shallow gasps of air kept her stomach from emptying.

She took a close-up shot of white powdered nostrils. ODs from cocaine didn't make much sense. Kate turned and stared at the mirror and razor blade that had been toppled from the coffee table. "Tim, we need to be looking for something besides coke that these kids stuck up their noses."

Tim stood beside the couch, dictating notes into his digital recorder. "Why do you say that?" he asked.

"These kids collapsed in the same room. If they had become excitable or agitated, they'd be all over the house. There's no vomit anywhere. At least I can't smell any. What's the drug of choice here in Scarborough?"

"Weed and alcohol, not much else around here. There's no extra money floating in people's bank accounts, especially since the furniture factory closed. Most of our families are living on unemployment."

"This family has money."

"Yeah, this is Pemberly Bowling's house—well Pemberly Wilks now."

"That's Pemberly? I didn't recognize her at all. She's Virginia blue blood, trust fund money. What did she say happened? Does she have any clues?"

"She said Chad wasn't feeling well. He called to tell her he had a bad headache. She told him to send his friends home, go up to the medicine cabinet, and get himself a couple of pain relievers."

"Has anyone checked the medicine cabinet?" Kate asked.

"You are. Pemberly said she keeps all the medicines in her bathroom."

Kate followed the curved mahogany stairwell up to the second floor. The oriental carpeting underfoot was slippery in her booties. She peaked around the doors until she reached the master suite and walked into the white marble bathroom. It was pristine—not a towel on the floor or a stray hair in the sink.

In the bathroom cabinet, Kate found the usual array of over-the-counter bottles and boxes, nothing that someone could cut into a white powder. When she moved the Pepto to the side, she found three prescription bottles. She picked up the one for Nardil and took a picture of the label. Thinking she'd look up the drug later when she got home, Kate carefully opened the bottle and tapped a pill into the lid.

Orange, not white. This probably won't matter. Kate snapped a photo. The next was for Cephalexin, the pharmacy date made it only a week old. Kate took a picture of the capsule and wondered why anyone would snort antibiotics. The third bottle made Kate's heart stutter. OxyContin. The same doctor who wrote the prescription for the Cephalexin was listed on the label. He had given Pemberly fourteen pills. "Take twice a day as needed for pain."

If Pemberly took them on schedule, there should be one left. Kate unscrewed the cap and stared at nine pills. A suspicion niggled in her brain, but she couldn't quite figure out why or what it was exactly. She took several pictures of the tablets, and then shouted, "Tim, I have something to show you."

⌶⌶⌶

"Pemberly, no one is blaming you for anything. We're just trying to account for the medications in the house," Tim said. "Seven days ago, you were given prescriptions for antibiotics and pain killers."

"Yes, I was up at the Country Club, and Bitsy Blanton backed into me with her golf cart. Ran right over my leg. The ambulance took me to the hospital. Nothing was broken, just a bad bruise. I was in terrible pain. And I needed five stitches."

"Did you follow the prescription on your antibiotics?"

"Yes, tonight's my last dose." Pemberly's limbs sagged from her body as if she was disintegrating in the sun, her words flat and lifeless.

"What about the pain medication?" Tim asked.

Kate hovered in the background, listening.

"Oh, I only took one of them. I got by on Tylenol. I felt so strange when I took the one from Doctor Michaels. I could hardly breathe. I almost called 9-1-1."

"You decided not to call?" Tim asked.

"I fell asleep. I slept for the longest time. When I woke up, I was better."

Tim glanced at the EMT. "Does she have someone on the way?"

"Her sister should be here soon. Her husband is trying to get a flight. He lives in Charlotte."

"Pemberly, you said you took one of the pills. There are nine left in the bottle. Have you any idea what happened to the four we haven't accounted for?"

Pemberly shook her head.

Two cars barreled down the road. Tim turned to Kate. "Seems the other family has been notified. We need to go back in the house and see if we can find those four pills."

....

THREE

A unt Emma sat in her sunny kitchen, muttering over the jumble from the morning paper when Kate walked in and headed straight for the coffee pot.

"You look like you're dressed to go to the station," Aunt Emma said without looking up.

Kate glanced down at her navy polo shirt and khaki BDUs she had picked up at the military surplus shop. Not her usual style, but she thought she should be in something that resembled a uniform if she was shadowing Tim.

"Tim's working on the case from yesterday, and I had some thoughts I wanted to share."

"It's front page news. You don't have to be so circumspect. Two little babies not even out of high school. They're saying drug overdose."

"I'm not allowed to comment. I'm sorry, Aunt Emma."

"No need. A tragedy is a tragedy. But it won't stop folks from heading up to Scarborough Knoll for the pig-picking. It'll be good for people to share their grief. It's not going to be the fun-filled hoo-ha that the Scarboroughs planned to help sway people to their side of the fence, though."

"Are you going?" Kate asked.

"I am, maybe a little later. I'm not so interested in the politics and the propaganda. I wanted the picketers and news crews to get hot and leave before I go."

"That's about the mining? I saw a bunch of signs on my drive into town."

"It's a shame the Scarboroughs found the uranium vein on their land. We all got along so much better before this. Now it's a house divided. You're either pro-mining or against it. In this economy with folks so desperate, it's not a pretty fight."

"Which side are you on?"

"I'm on Owen's side. And Owen didn't want uranium to poison his great granddaddy's land."

"This land? Why would Uncle Owen be worried about that? This is uphill from the Knoll; any runoff would affect the valley between the two properties, and the Scarboroughs own that."

"I can't say that I have a proper answer for you. I didn't pay much attention. There was something about needing a holding pond in this direction, away from the riverfront to meet some standards. It doesn't matter none. Owen said no. And if they ask me, I'll say no, as well. And right now, mining isn't legal anyway."

"Well, I'm heading into town. You enjoy your soft-serve ice cream." Kate rinsed her mug and set it on the drying rack. She turned and kissed her aunt's forehead. "Thank you for the coffee."

Aunt Emma reached for Kate's hand. "You talked to him this morning?"

Kate shook her head. "I talked to his buddy Zack. Ryan put his fist through a wall. They took him to the emergency room. Nothing's broken, except the wall, that is."

Aunt Emma nodded. "This is a small town, and you like your privacy. People are going to see those red rings around your eyes and wonder what's wrong. Wonder turns to speculation, and speculation becomes fact quicker than a flash of lightning."

"I know, and I'm sure this won't be the last time I look this bad. I already decided to blame it on my allergies to your cat."

"But I don't have a cat, dear."

"You will tonight. I'm stopping by the shelter on the way home. Do you have a color preference?"

⌙⌙⌣⌣⌐⌐

"Good, you're here. Come on. I want to introduce you to everyone." Tim strode down the corridor on long legs. He had been the high school quarterback when Kate was in school. He'd probably put his running skills to good use on the streets, keeping the townspeople safe. But now that he was a detective, he wore a jacket and tie, and he probably left the full body contact to the uniforms.

Kate followed him into the conference room. Officers filled the chairs in neat rows, all of them dressed with military precision. Kate glanced around, but found no other women.

She focused on her boots, trying to still the butterflies in her stomach. Being the focus of attention was a work-a-day reality in the classroom, but the vibe Kate picked up here was that these guys didn't want her invading their man cave.

"Gentlemen." As Tim spoke, the room settled down to respectful silence. "I would like to introduce you to Kate Hamilton. Mrs. Hamilton is a science teacher in Boston. As part of her continuing education requirements, she's taken classes to accomplish a second diploma—this one in Crime Scene Sciences. She's here fulfilling the internship requirements. When she returns home, Mrs. Hamilton plans to use her knowledge to encourage her students' love of science, and maybe a few of them will aspire to joining us good guys in our fight against crime. Mrs. Hamilton will be helping me for the next few months. She comes to us with the latest techniques, and I plan to take full advantage of her while she's here."

A cough from the back of the room sounded like a veiled "I bet."

Tim either didn't hear or pointedly ignored the interruption. "Let's give her a warm welcome."

The men clapped, but it didn't feel very warm to Kate.

"Are there any questions before Sergeant takes over with today's briefing?" Tim asked.

One of the officers laced his hands behind his head and leaned back in his chair, stretching out his legs. "Why did you come *here,* to our little hick town? Seems like if you wanted to see crime close up, you could've stayed in Boston." The menace in his voice was unmistakable.

Kate recognized him as Ken Arthur, Doris' brother. She'd dealt with the bullies in her classroom, so she knew she'd need to take the upper hand immediately, or she'd be fighting him from here on.

"Well, Officer Arthur," she smiled sweetly as if unperturbed, "I'm killing two birds with one stone."

Ken Arthur sat straight up, his hands making fists on his knees. "Now what's that supposed to mean?"

The door opened slightly, and a woman stuck her head into the room. "Detective?"

Tim gave her a nod. "Gentlemen," he said to the room, then turned on his heel and walked out, with Kate trailing behind him.

"What've you got, Helen?"

"There's a woman on the phone, says she's a nurse up at the hospital. Jennifer Baker. She came home from the night shift and found her kids' beds still made. She says that means no one slept in them last night."

"How many kids? How old?"

"Her two sons. They're sixteen—twins."

"Have you sent a patrol to talk with her?"

"No, I thought you might want to go yourself. Mrs. Baker says she read in the paper about the teens dying at the Wilks' house. She said her boys were good friends with Chad Wilks."

"Helen, get me the…"

Helen held out a post-it note with an address written on it in capital letters.

Kate buckled her seatbelt and swiveled to see Tim's face. He bent forward, turned the key in the ignition, and slid the air conditioning lever to high.

"Did you notice anything unusual about the OxyContin pills yesterday?"

"No, why?" He put his arm across the seat and twisted to back out of the parking space.

"I was looking at the pictures I took at the crime scene last night. Did you send the last of the pills on to the medical examiner's office?"

"I did." They stopped at the road, waiting for a break in traffic. Tim watched Kate rub the heel of her palm into her forehead. "Uh oh. I know that gesture. Everything out of your mouth now is going to be bad news."

"There were four pills missing. If we assumed the boys used one pill each, that leaves two unaccounted for."

"And two boys missing. You're jumping to conclusions. That's not what a scientist does, and it's certainly not what a detective does. You need to collect evidence and then try to see the pattern, not create a pattern and try to fill it in with evidence."

"I'm not officially a CSI until Monday. I'm telling you what my teacher's gut is saying. I bet you anything that when we have access to those kids' phones, we'll find two things. One, that someone Googled how to get high on OxyContin; and two, that one of the dead kids either called or texted the two boys that are missing. Remember that Pemberly said she told Chad to send his friends home. Friends, plural. We only found one friend."

Tim flipped his lights on to go around a tractor-trailer. "There's more," he said. "Stop drip feeding me."

"OxyContin is the prescription name for Oxycodone. Do you know much about that drug?"

"They use it for long term pain management for cancer patients and the like. It's from the opiate family. Abuse was a real problem for counties further west of us out toward Bristol, though, you hear about it less and less. We haven't had trouble with it here."

"Okay, well, Pemberly's prescription threw up all kinds of flags you should consider."

"Go on."

"The strength stamped on the pills was 80mg. The usual dosage is 40 mg or less. Anything over 40mg is for opioid-tolerant patients only. As a matter of fact, a dose of 80mg in a day can be lethal to someone who hasn't built up resistance."

"There's an interesting piece of information. So Pemberly's prescription was a potentially lethal dose?"

"Yes, unless she was used to using opioids. Maybe you should get a look at her medical records. Here's another flag: the pills were stamped OC. They should have been stamped OP."

"You think her meds got mixed up?"

"Something very bizarre is going on. You see, the formulation of the pills allows the ingredients to be time-released over twelve hours. The druggies couldn't get a good high because of the time-release component. They found if they crushed the pills, they

28

could snort them or shoot them and take the full hit of the narcotic all at once. That was with the first formulation, the OC pills."

"But you said they're supposed to be stamped OP." The muscles in Tim's face became taut with concentration.

"People OD'ed in a large enough quantity that the FDA considered pulling Oxycodone. The pharmaceutical company reformulated it so when a druggy tried to powder the pill to get around the time-release component, all they got was goo. That goo can't be snorted or shot-up. The new formulation is stamped OP. With the OC off the market, druggies turned to easier highs."

"But these were OC pills. And because the pill was a potentially lethal quantity when time-released, we can assume a full dose, shot directly into a teenager's system, would be sure death," Tim said.

Kate rubbed the back of her hand. "That's the conclusion I came to last night."

"Could the pharmacy be dispensing the old pills until they're gone, and then replace them with the new ones?"

"I sincerely doubt it. The formulation change took place a long time ago."

"What's a long time look like?" Tim asked.

"Eighteen months or so. The street price for an 80mg OC pill would be astronomical. You simply can't find them anymore. I would assume the pharmaceutical reps came through, picked up the OC, and swapped them with OP. Even if that weren't true, most meds have a shelf life of about a year. The pill's sell-by date should have expired, and they'd be destroyed."

"These pills should have lost their potency by now?"

"Some of their potency, but obviously not enough."

"And you know this how?" Tim asked.

"I took my final exam in Narcotics and Substance Abuse in May. I checked my notes on my computer when I got home last night."

"Holy hell. We need to find out if the pharmacy has distributed these pills to anyone else."

"I would. Where are the teens' autopsies being done?"

"Roanoke."

"Oh." Kate turned her attention to the ramshackle houses strung along the railroad tracks as they passed by. The whole town had disintegrated since she'd last been here. Poverty was evidenced in peeling paint and sagging rooflines. The yards were overgrown with weeds; no money for lawn mower gas. "When will you have the official cause of death?"

Tim signaled a right turn. "Toxicology reports usually take two to four weeks, so it'll be a while before we have anything definitive."

Kate gripped her knees. "Do you think the two missing boys are dead?" She sucked her lips in as soon as the words passed her teeth. ·

"Just between you and me, Katie, I've got a bad feeling we're too late. I sure hope I'm wrong about this. Four high schoolers dead in a week is a hell of a loss for a small town like Scarborough."

"And Uncle Owen. That sure is a lot of dying in a short span."

Tim eased the squad car off the side of the road. The children's mother stood in the driveway, wringing her hands.

As they popped the doors open, the woman, dressed in blue scrubs, squatted next to her car, one hand stretched to the ground for stability the other fisted at her chest, sobbing. Tim put in a call for a paramedic. "Here we go," he said, climbing from the car.

FOUR

....

Mrs. Baker," Tim crouched beside her. "Ma'am, I know you're scared. But if your boys are in trouble, they need you right now. I have to have some answers so I can find them."

Kate pushed some Kleenexes into the woman's hand. Mrs. Baker pulled them across her face, smearing snot onto her cheek.

"They're big boys. They're good boys." Tim's voice had a solid quality to it that said Mrs. Baker could lean on him, and he would support her. "They're probably having an adventure, and we need to get them home. Do they have phones? Did you try calling them?"

Mrs. Baker nodded and pointed toward the house; she opened her mouth, but a belch and sob came out with no information.

"Kate, why don't you walk Mrs. Baker to the patrol car? See if you can get her comfortable in the air conditioning. It's climbing toward a hundred today."

Tim handed her the keys, then tugged on a pair of gloves as he trekked to the house.

Kate pulled Mrs. Baker's arm around her shoulder and power-lifted the woman to a standing position. She led her to the car and seated her in the back. Reaching into the Igloo, Kate pulled out one of Tim's water bottles and opened the top.

"Here, Mrs. Baker, take a sip. You'll feel better." Kate guided the woman's hands to hold the bottle. "You told the operator that Chad and your sons were good friends?"

She nodded.

"Then you knew Chad very well. This must be terrifying for you." Kate struggled to find the right words. "And as hard as it is to work around those feelings, you understand, the more information we have, the faster we can bring your boys home. When did you see them last?"

Jennifer Baker tipped the whole bottle down. When she came up for air, she seemed to have wrestled her emotions into control. She rubbed the back of her wrist across her chin to catch the water drops. "I saw them yesterday morning. But I talked to them around three in the afternoon, and they were fine. I went to the gym, and then I met a friend for pizza and a movie before I went to work. I was on seven to seven last night. I'm late getting home because of all the paperwork they have us fill out at the end of each shift."

"Are you a single mom? Or was there another adult in the house?"

34

"Their daddy drives a truck. He's somewhere near Ohio right about now."

Kate nodded. "When you talked to your sons at three, did you talk to one of them, or both?"

"Each of them. I told them they had to get their chores done before they went out, and they had to be home before dark. They needed to put the trash can down by the mailbox and unload the dishwasher." Mrs. Baker squeezed her eyelids tightly shut.

Kate looked up to see a bin set out at the end of the driveway.

"You said they had to be home by dark." Kate touched Mrs. Baker's hand so she would open her eyes. "Where were they going?"

"Out. They'd meet friends by the river and go floating on inner tubes, sometimes catch some fish and fry them up on a fire. Nothing much."

"Do they have their own car?" Kate asked, watching as Tim strode toward them.

"No, they probably walked unless one of their friends picked them up."

Tim opened the car door and stuck his head in. "Do your boys usually go far without their phones?"

"They don't take them down to the river. I told them if these phones got damaged, they wouldn't get new ones."

"Is there any place else they wouldn't take them?"

35

"No, sir. Usually those phones are like another appendage."

"Ma'am, you can go in your house now and get comfortable. Search and Rescue is on the way. They're bringing the bloodhounds, so we should be able to track them right quick. Is there someone we can call to sit with you?"

"I can call someone," she said.

After Mrs. Baker settled herself on the couch, clinging to her neighbor's hand, Kate and Tim headed outside.

"You've slapped that impassive mask right across your face, Tim. I always hated when you did that."

Tim pursed his lips. "As soon as the sergeant gets here, we're moving on."

"You don't do detective work on missing kids?"

"I talked to my supervisor about what you told me. He did some quick research while I was on the phone, and you were right about all of it. The formulation change would never have come up in an autopsy report. We would have chalked this up to kids making a bad mistake. Cause of death would be accidental."

"But now?"

"Now someone's liable. What the charges will be depends on what our investigation turns up."

"Do you think someone wanted to kill Pemberly on purpose, or do you think this was some kind of horrible mistake?"

Tim moved to his side of the car. "You're doing it again."

"What?" She burned her fingertips on the door handle; it was so hot.

Tim reached in and cranked the air conditioning to blow the heat out of the car. Neither of them attempted to get in. "Don't hypothesize. Get a panoramic view, and then start to narrow your scope down until you've caught the bad guy in your crosshairs."

Standing beside the car, she was damp with perspiration. Kate pulled her long brown hair into a ponytail and twisted it around until it made a bun. She used her pen to hold the mess in place, and then tried to catch her reflection in the back window to see if she had any semblance of a professional appearance.

"Cute as a bug, Katydid," Tim said.

Kate froze for a millisecond. Her heart pounded against her rib cage, then slowed as she realized it was an old habit. He hadn't meant anything personal by it.

An unmarked car pulled up behind them. Tim sauntered back to talk to the sergeant, and Kate slid into their car. The interior was like a furnace. She turned the vent's blast directly onto her overheated face as she waited for him to return.

"You need some oil for those cogs whirring in your brain. They're squeaking," Kate said. "Where are we headed?"

"Dogwood Pharmacy. That's where Pemberly had her prescription filled."

"Do you have a search warrant?"

"Not yet, they're in the works. I want to do a quick check-see on their OxyContin supply and make sure no one else has the old formula. We should have a judge's signature soon."

The rest of their ride was in silence. Kate chewed on the inside of her cheek and watched the cows lolling in their pastures. Just on the outskirts of town, Tim pulled up in front of Country Kitchen. Kate turned a questioning gaze on him.

"It's a might early for lunch, but why don't you take the opportunity? And if you wouldn't mind, order something for me."

"You're not coming in?"

Tim blushed ever so slightly. "I'll do the pharmacy run by myself. Doris Arthur is the owner now, and I might have better luck if you weren't with me."

"I noticed her giving me the evil eye at the funeral. I haven't seen her since high school graduation. What could I possibly have done to rile her up? And her brother, too, for that matter."

38

The blush grew brighter, and Tim flicked his eyes away. "I couldn't say for sure."

Kate opened the door and stuck her foot out. "You always were a terrible liar. What do you want me to order for you?"

"What I always get." His smile was sheepish and a little bit relieved.

╫╫╫

Kate gazed at the menu board. It was too early in the day for her to feel hungry.

"The chicken salad is good."

Kate turned to find Dr. Omid Javarti standing behind her.

"They make it with dried cherries and walnuts," he continued. "It's quite refreshing with a glass of lemonade."

Kate gave him a polite smile. "Thank you, that does sound good. How are you? You're not on duty at the hospital today?"

"I work seven days on, seven days off. Today starts my week of rest."

"Wow, I'd like that schedule." Kate stepped up to the cashier and ordered her lunch. "And may I have a double cheeseburger—no condiments, large fries, and a milkshake half vanilla, half chocolate to go?"

"Yes, ma'am. Do you want me to hold off putting that together until you're almost done eating, so it's fresh?" The cashier was an apple-cheeked woman with an ample bosom resting on her over-broad stomach.

"I'd appreciate that." Kate paid and moved to a seat near the window to watch for Tim's return.

"Mind if I join you?" Dr. Javarti asked, his hand resting on the back of the wooden chair.

"Please."

"How is your aunt doing?" He unrolled his cutlery from the paper napkin.

"Outwardly, she's fine, thank you."

"And inwardly?"

"I would never know. Aunt Emma and stoicism are synonymous."

"I was serious about her health. If you see her needing a medicinal crutch for the time being, please call me. I want her to be as comfortable as possible under these circumstances. I don't mind writing her a prescription."

"Thank you kindly. I'll remember that." Kate took in Dr. Javarti's appearance. Even on this smoldering day, he had on dark pants with sharp pleats. He wore his hair cut short with a long bang that he swept back, and he sported the stylized five o'clock shadow popular with the fashionable crowds in Boston. This man belonged in New York City, not Podunk, Virginia.

"What?" He laughed.

"Sorry, I just… I can't figure out how in the world you found yourself here. Where are you from originally?"

"Originally? Ahh. So, you want me to tell you a story?"

"Yes, please," Kate said as the cashier brought them their drinks.

"I was born in Karaj, Iran. When I was thirteen, my parents sent me to America to spend the summer with my aunt and uncle to improve my English. My parents disappeared soon after. So my aunt's family adopted me, and I became an American citizen. I went to college, followed by medical school and residency, and then returned home, where I became a professor at the University. And that, as they say here in Scarborough, is it in a nutshell."

"Karaj to Scarborough? That's quite a leap."

"Not as far as you would think. Besides the obvious incentives of my hospital paycheck, which greatly supersedes the paltry amount of money I garnered as a professor, I did my undergraduate work at Virginia Tech. I love the rolling hills and shades of green found here in Virginia. And I became quite a fishing addict."

"Fish?"

"Catfish."

Kate laughed. "I guess there aren't many catfish in Karaj." The waitress set thick white pottery plates in front of them. Kate spread her napkin across her lap.

"You said your parents disappeared. Were they ever found again?" Kate's hand shot out, and she touched Dr. Javarti's forearm. "I'm sorry, that was rude. It popped out of my mouth before I could stop it."

"It's natural to be curious," Dr. Javarti took a bite of his sandwich; after swallowing, he said, "I actually returned home to find them. I hoped they were dead."

Kate's eyes flashed wide.

"It sounds callous. I can see you're horrified. Let me explain. My parents were very forward thinking. They were both part of the intelligentsia. My father was a professor of nuclear sciences, and my mother held a PhD in philosophy—both were educated in America. At Harvard, as a matter of fact." Dr. Javarti took a long drink from his glass. "I love lemonade," he said, pausing. "After they finished their degrees, they returned home. They wanted to be part of the new Iran, and hoped the policies coming out of Tehran would vault our country into the modern age, where women would have significance in society. Both of my parents wanted to help move Iran toward equal rights for women."

"And they had you. Do you have any siblings?"

42

"No. I was a much doted-upon only child, which is how I came to be in America. My parents had information that the authorities had marked them for reprisal, and brought me here to keep me safe."

"But they returned home?"

"Yes, equality was their cause to fight, and they needed to be fully engaged. Soon after their return, the SAVAK picked them up and leveled our house to the ground."

"The SAVAK?"

"That was the Shah's secret police force."

"Oh, my." Kate laid her hand over her heart. "Dr. Javarti, I'm so sorry."

"Omid, please. And yes, it was a great loss for my country and for me personally."

"Now you're back in rural Virginia, fishing for catfish and enduring the humidity."

"The humidity is very hard, indeed. I am used to desert heat. This..." he held his hands up as if supporting something physically heavy, "...robs me of my energy."

"Did you retire from teaching?" Kate asked, taking a bite of her sandwich. "Are you back here permanently?"

"A three-year sabbatical. I'm a hospitalist and have a contract with the management company, which found me exactly the kind of assignment I was looking for: a sleepy little town in need of a doctor, with plenty of time to enjoy catfishing." He smiled.

"It must be a very exciting time in the Middle East with the Arab Spring and all of the changes."

"Yet another reason to find myself comfortably hidden away in Southwest Virginia."

"Oh?" Kate put her sandwich back on the plate.

"Holding an American passport, and coming from my family's activist history, my presence at the University was receiving a great deal of scrutiny. After a private word with some people in-the-know, I decided that a sabbatical was in my best interest." Omid cleared his throat. "Having told you my life story, I'm entitled to one or two questions of my own, don't you think?"

"All right." Kate said, reaching for her glass.

"Your aunt told me that you came to visit for the summer."

"I have. I'm finishing up some school work. I'm a teacher normally, but I've been studying crime scene investigation. It's very popular with the teens. I wanted to find a less daunting way to get my female students engaged in sciences so they will consider science as a viable career path."

Omid nodded. "My mother also pushed for girls to go into the sciences. It was a great passion of hers."

Kate read something odd about his body language. Was it shame? Anger? She could understand anger.

"So, are you doing an internship with the police department?" he asked. "Is that why you're here?"

"I am. I'm also here to spend time with my aunt."

"A terrible tragedy, the children's deaths. It's all anyone could talk about this morning at the party on the Knoll. Are you working on that case? I understand they died when they snorted lines of adulterated coke."

"I'm sorry, Omid. I'm not at liberty to discuss the particulars of the case." Kate felt someone staring at her and turned suddenly to discover whom. Behind her stood Custis Scarborough. He stalked over.

"Hello, Doc."

Custis' eyes glimmered maliciously; a sneer masqueraded as a smile. When Kate's spine juddered, Omid reached out to cover her hand protectively.

"What do you want, Custis?" she asked.

"Just being polite. Came over to say hey. I heard you were back in town. Plan to be here long?"

"My plans haven't been set in stone."

The bell jingled, and Tim stepped in. Kate yanked her hand away from Omid and hid it in her lap.

45

Custis nodded at Tim. "Nice to see you, Detective. Looks like you've got yourself a little competition." He glanced down at Kate. "I'll catch up with you. We've got unfinished business."

"No, we don't," Kate said, finally getting herself back under control. "Everything that needed to be said was said. I'd prefer you keep your distance."

Custis ran his tongue across his teeth. "I bet you would."

Tim stood behind her chair. "Custis," he said with a nod. "Surprised to see you in town today. Thought you'd be busy up at your pig-picking."

"Just running a quick errand for Mama. We're having a blast. Hope to see you up there with your family when your shift's over. We plan to have music into the night. Got a big ol' bonfire ready and marshmallows for the kids to roast. Your boys would have a great time—and Pam." With that, Custis dipped his head to give Kate a wink.

The two men had squared off, the pleasantries barely masking their disdain. The cashier waddled over and looked from face to face, before she set a brown paper bag and a Styrofoam cup beside Kate's plate and left without a word.

"Thank you for the company, Omid." Kate pushed up from the table. "Enjoy the rest of your lunch."

46

Tim held the door wide for Kate. His lower jaw thrust out, making him look pugnacious. As soon as they were in the privacy of the car, Kate expected the inquisition to begin. She was wrong.

A call went out over the radio for any units in the vicinity of High Street to respond to a medical emergency; the paramedics' ETA was fifteen minutes.

"Buckle up. That's us. We're only a mile away." Tim responded to the dispatcher, tapped his lights and siren on, and jetted down the road.

FIVE

....

Tim raced from the car, up the flower-lined stairs, and through the wide open door. Kate ran right behind him, grabbing at the handrail to keep from stumbling. Tim looked left, then right into the dining room and living room. "Police," he shouted. He pointed Kate towards the back of the house as he took the stairs two at a time to check the bedrooms.

"Here," Kate hollered as she came upon the elderly woman hunkered over her husband, trying to blow life back into his lungs.

Kate rounded the couple and pressed two fingers against the man's carotid artery. She couldn't find a pulse.

Tim pounded down the staircase.

"Kitchen," she yelled, throwing her leg over the man and positioning herself for CPR. Her hands shook as she stacked them and interlaced her fingers. She thrust down with her strength and weight. Tim pulled the woman from her spot and took over the breaths.

Four cycles in and sweat coursed down Kate's back. Her strength waned along with her original burst of adrenaline.

"On three, we switch," Tim said then lowered with another breath.

Kate plunged down, counting aloud. "One, two, three."

She rolled to the right, and Tim took over. Kate tilted the elderly man's head back. "Could he be choking?" Kate asked the woman as she squeezed his nostrils, then covered his lips with her own.

"Asthma attack. He was still talking when I found him." The woman clutched the front of her dress.

Kate counted the CPR thrusts to time her breaths. She watched Tim's powerful arms; they never waned, never sputtered.

As the EMTs jogged into the room, pushed the table and chairs out of the way, and used their equipment to register any sign of life, Tim and Kate continued their efforts. One of the responders pulled back the man's eyelid and touched his eyeball. There was no reflex.

The paramedic put his hand on Kate's shoulder. "Ma'am, it's okay to stop now. I'm calling it. Time of death, twelve twenty-six."

A wail rose up in the woman's throat and coursed through Kate's veins like an electrical current, lighting her nerves on fire. Two women, hovering at the door opening, rushed forward to gather up the new widow into their arms.

Tim pulled his phone from his pocket as Kate moved to the sink to wash her hands and catch her breath.

The EMTS packed up to leave. The women followed after them.

Kate was drying her hands on a dishtowel when the elderly woman, Rebecca Brody, came back in alone.

"Mrs. Brody, I'm sorry for your loss," Tim began.

"I want to thank you both. You did what you could. I guess the Good Lord needed Wayne at his side. He's gone home."

"Yes, ma'am. Mrs. Brody, this is Kate Hamilton, she's working with me for the summer."

"I barely got off the phone, when you were at my door. When I found him, Wayne was still breathing." Mrs. Brody spread her arms wide and let them flop to her side. "Then all of a sudden, nothing. I only got one breath in him. I could never have done what you did. Oh, you must be exhausted. Please come and sit down."

"We're okay, ma'am, thank you. I've called the funeral home, and they're on the way. Because this was an unexpected death, it will be up to the coroner whether they do an autopsy or not."

"Can I cover him?" she asked, pulling a tablecloth from the drawer.

"Yes, ma'am." Tim grabbed hold of the bottom and helped Mrs. Brody. "You said asthma. Did your husband have a history of asthma attacks?"

"I'm *assuming* that's what it was. Wayne has...had...Wayne had rather severe bronchial asthma. But I don't know for sure. I wasn't here, you see. I was at the grocery store. I brought in the first bag." She pointed to the floor by the table where a brown paper bag laid on its side. "Wayne was gasping for air. I grabbed up his rescue inhaler and helped him spray it into his mouth, but he wasn't taking deep enough breaths for it to be of any use. I called 9-1-1 and tried to calm him down. Then he was on the floor and not breathing anymore." Mrs. Brody stared at the mound where her husband lay. Kate realized the woman was still in shock. Not a tear was on her face.

Tim stood back and scanned the room. Kate followed suit. Lunch was on the table. A peanut butter and jelly sandwich with chips, and a glass of orange juice. A laptop was set up next to the half-eaten sandwich, but the screen was dark. Tim walked over, wrapped his finger with a napkin, and tapped the space bar. A word document came up.

Tim scanned the page. "Mrs. Brody, the whole town is up at Scarborough Knoll today. Were you and Mr. Brody going there later?"

"Oh, no. We would never do that. Wayne is an environmental engineer, and he stands…" her breath caught, and she steadied herself on the wall before she continued, "he *stood* in staunch opposition to uranium mining. That's probably what got him riled up into such a state - all that propaganda going on over at Scarborough Knoll."

Mrs. Brody sat down in the kitchen chair. Her hand reached out as she spoke, and she touched and moved things around. Kate wondered if she was aware of what she was doing. Mrs. Brody's voice compressed like she was forcing words from a tight space. "The Scarborough family is right excited. They think in the next round of votes, the legislature will lift the moratorium on uranium mining. That's what Wayne was working on there. He was writing his opposition paper to give to Senator Orly." Mrs. Brody reached out a hand to point to the computer, but her finger hit the glass and sent orange juice dripping from the table.

Kate rushed forward with the kitchen towel to wipe up the mess, and then she crouched to blot the carpet. She tugged a latex glove from her side pocket and wriggled it on. She stood up holding an inhaler and a prescription bottle. OxyContin 80mg. She held it out for Tim to see.

Tim pulled on a pair of gloves and opened the childproof top. There were five OC- 80mg tablets inside the bottle. He looked at the label, and his face went impassive. "Ma'am, has your husband sought help for pain recently?" he asked.

"The fool put his back out two weeks ago, trying to move the blasted piano all by himself. I had to get the ambulance up here to take him to the hospital. He couldn't walk."

"And they issued a prescription for the pain?"

"Yes, some pain pills. But my daughter-in-law is a chiropractor. She came in and worked on him, and he said he was mostly better and didn't need the medication."

"There's only one missing. Do you think he took it today?"

"I told him he should."

"And why was that, ma'am?" Tim put the lid back in place.

"He'd been hunkered over that computer for hours yesterday, and was up moaning most of the night. When I went to the grocery store, I handed him the bottle and said if he started hurting, he should consider taking one."

"Do you mind if I hold on to this bottle?"

"Of course not, but why would you want it?"

"Routine procedure, ma'am."

Kate brought Mrs. Brody's groceries in. The frozen foods had melt-ed, and the milk had already turned sour. She put what was salvageable in the fridge while Tim was in the cruiser conferencing with his boss. Mr. Brody's body was on the way to the morgue. Mrs. Brody's friends filed in, and Kate felt better about leaving. She offered her sympathy, said her goodbyes, and then went to join Tim.

"Got her settled?"

"The cavalry's arrived."

"Yup, probably only took this long because the word had to get to the Knoll."

"It's crazy how dead the whole town is today."

A smile spread over Tim's face. "Katydid, was that gallows humor?"

"More like a poor choice of words. Are you going to tell me what you found out at the pharmacy?"

"I didn't get much, because of HIPPA. I need to get those warrants in hand before we see anything. I'm heading back there now with Wayne Brody's prescription."

"Not much, but something?" Kate stretched around. "I'm grabbing one of your water bottles. Do you want one?"

"Don't you have my lunch somewhere?"

Kate reached down and pulled out the bag. "It's bound to be gross. Your shake is melted."

"Hand me that. Half and half?"

"Of course."

He sent her a wink. "I knew you'd remember."

The heat of her blush spread across Kate's face. She turned quickly so Tim wouldn't see. She took in the tree-lined street with the picture-perfect white picket fences. Deep porches flew American flags and held swings with colorful pillows. This wasn't a place where bad things should happen.

She sent a quick glance Tim's way. "You were telling me about the pharmacy?"

"They keep special paperwork on the distribution of all narcotics. There are laws that apply specifically to that class of drugs. I asked Doris to take a look and tell me when she last filled a prescription for OxyContin. She said it was February."

"Both Pemberly's and Wayne's prescriptions were filled this month."

"Thank you, Doctor Watson."

"Did you check their OxyContin supply?" Kate asked.

"Doris showed me. The highest dosage she carries right now is 20mg. She can order a higher concentration if someone needs it. And it's all OP."

56

"Did you ask…"

"When it was switched out? Yes ma'am, I did. She said it happened about Halloween time, a year and a half ago."

"How weird is that?"

"Pretty darned weird."

Kate noticed Tim's knuckles whiten as he gripped the steering wheel.

"Are you ready for some bad news?" he asked.

"Oh, no." Kate covered her face with her hands.

"Yeah, Search and Rescue found the boys' bodies down at the river. They had a mirror and razor blade." Tim paused and worked his jaw. "They'd been dead for quite a while. In this heat with all them bugs down there, things progressed pretty far." He glanced over at her. "I'm glad you didn't find them."

Tears dripped down Kate's cheeks, but she reigned in the sob that swelled in her throat. Their poor mother. Even though it was her job to help with such a scene, Kate agreed with Tim: she was glad she hadn't found the boys. These teens reminded her of her students at home and filled Kate's heart with pain.

Tim shoved the gear into park. He patted her knee. "Katie, you stay here. Drink some water. I'm going in to talk to Doris."

....

SIX

"Aunt Emma, I'm home."

"Oh, honey. Come here. You've had a terrible day. I heard about your trying to save Wayne Brody."

Kate drifted into the kitchen.

"Why, what have you got there?" Aunt Emma asked, tying her apron around her waist.

"This is your new kitty. You didn't tell me what color, so I picked a gray. Do you like him?"

"Oh, so tiny. This is just a baby." Aunt Emma gathered the kitten against her chest and tickled her fingers through its silky fur. "Owen just hated cats. Hated them. I never even asked if I could bring one home."

"Is this okay?"

"Yes, dear. Lovely. And look, a little boy. I'll call him Bingley." She dropped a kiss on the top of the kitten's head.

"Ha! I never took you for a romantic." Kate went to sit at the table. "You're a Jane Austen fan?"

Aunt Emma gave her a confused glance. "Is there a woman alive who isn't? Thank you, honey. I love him already. Here, let me fetch you a glass of sweet tea."

"Thank you." Kate sat down while her aunt poured. "I talked to Ryan today."

"Is he feeling better? How's his hand?" Aunt Emma handed Kate the glass then adjusted Bingley up onto to her shoulder. He rumbled with satisfaction as Aunt Emma's fingers massaged over him.

"You got a kitty, and he got his dog today. It's a black lab. A female." Kate took a gulp from glass and shuddered as her system took a full hit of the syrupy sweetness. "He named her Houston."

"Houston? That's a strange name for a girl dog, isn't it?"
"His sense of humor, 'Houston, we have a problem.'"

"Do you think the dog will help?"

"Lord, I hope so. But no, it's just a piece of the puzzle—meds, therapy, his marine buddies, puppy, and time."

"Katherine, look at me."

Kate moved her gaze from her lap to her aunt's face.

"Things have progressed a far piece since the Vietnam War. People are different, care is different, and Owen sure never had a dog to help him. There's hope."

Kate sucked in a deep breath. "That's what I keep telling myself. I love him. I really do. Truly. Deeply. But I'm not you, Aunt Emma. You have that corundum core."

"It's an inherited quality. I see it in you. You'll surprise yourself."

Kate pulled her lips in and shook her head. "I'm not sure we can survive this. He doesn't even want me in the same house with him right now."

Aunt Emma reached out and stroked her hair. "He's protecting you the best he can. He was right to ask you to go. It's too dangerous for you to be there. He needs to deal with this on his own."

⌐┐┌⌐

Being a former Prom Queen isn't a bulletproof vest. Watch your back.

Kate blinked at the text message that popped up. Ryan was thinking about her. He was concerned. It was oddly worded, but what did she care? She dialed her home phone and got a busy signal. *Darn.* Kate needed to hear her husband's voice. Needed some connection with him. She tried again.

"Do you need a minute?" Tim asked.

Kate hadn't seen him come up. "I was trying to reach Ryan. I'll catch him later." She slid her cell phone into the thigh pocket on her khaki BDUs. "What are we doing today?"

"We're heading over to the hospital. I have warrants to get copies of Pemberly Wilks and Wayne Brody's medical histories. I'm going to send a copy to the medical examiner's office. And I want to make an appointment for us to talk with Dr. Michaels about his role in all this."

"Because his name is on both of the OxyContin prescriptions?"

"Yes, and because he attended both of them in the emergency room. Then I'm going to drop you off at home. I want you to relax for the rest of the day. Tomorrow morning, we need to go to the first of the teens' funerals and see what we can see."

"What are you doing after you drop me off?"

Tim rubbed a finger over his lower lip. "I need to go to Dogwood Pharmacy. Now that I have a warrant, Doris can answer my questions."

"You won't bring her into the station for that?"

"I need her to access her computers. Besides, the records for Brody and Wilks, I need a list of employees. I also want the names of the people on duty when Wilks and Brody had their prescriptions filled."

"Okay, but I was doing a little research last night about Oxycodone and interactions," Kate said.

"And what did you find?"

"In my class, we learned that people die from Oxycodone because it represses the respiratory cycle. I wondered why any doctor who knew Wayne Brody had asthma would write a script for the drug. And if they wrote the script, why would a pharmacist fill it? Pharmacy computers have pop-up warnings to prevent drug interactions. Wayne Brody filled his inhaler and his OxyContin at Dogwood Pharmacy."

"Interesting point," Tim said.

"I have another one."

Tim chuckled. "Somehow I thought you would."

"Pemberly was taking Nardil. It's an anti-depressant and one of the drugs listed as a definite no-no for mixing with Oxycodone. Pemberly had her Nardil filled at Dogwood, also. That shouldn't be possible. The origin of the problem could have been the doctor making bad decisions. But because Dogwood's computer should have prevented the prescription from being filled, the proper paperwork for the authorities was not filled out, and they don't even seem to legitimately carry the drug, this all points to nefarious actions taking place at Dogwood."

"Nefarious actions? Kate, you're reading too many novels. But I will say those are reasonable conclusions to draw. I'll check into it."

....

SEVEN

"I'm in here," Aunt Emma called as Kate pushed open the front door.

Kate followed the voice back to the kitchen where she found her aunt putting together a blueberry cobbler. "Oh, yay. Do we have ice cream, too?" Kate asked, sticking her head in the freezer.

"It's there on the right. How was your day?" Aunt Emma spooned the berries into the casserole.

"Difficult. We went to the funeral for one of the teens this morning."

"Yes, I was there, too."

Kate took down two glasses. "Can I pour you some sweet tea?"

"That'd be fine."

"I didn't see you there," Kate said.

"No, but I saw you, and more importantly, I saw Pam Gibbons. Go ahead and sit yourself down. I want to have a talk with you."

Kate moved to the table and sat in one of the hard backed chairs. She got the same queasy stomach she used to get when she went to the principal's office in grammar school.

Aunt Emma perched on the chair across from her, their knees bumping. "Seems to me, young lady, you're sitting in a frying pan ready to jump into a fire. I just want to know if you're aware of what's going on around you."

"This has something to do with Pam?"

Bingley jumped up to join them. Aunt Emma reached over and plucked the kitten off the table. "She's scared to death."

"About all the people who are dying?" Kate reached for Bingley and nestled him into her lap.

"Lord no, why would she be scared about that? No, she's worried you've come back for Tim."

"Ow!" Kate yelled as the kitten's claws pricked through her khakis. She moved him to the floor where he became entranced with her bootlaces. Kate sat up to see the stern set of her aunt's eyebrow. "Oh, that's just silly. Tim and I were children when we dated."

"He asked you to marry him, Kate. You turned him down and left for college."

"Of course I did. I didn't want to be a cop's wife, and I sure didn't want to live in a small town for the rest of my life. He always knew I planned to leave town and live in the city."

"Everyone thought you loved him enough that you'd change your mind. He surely did."

"Now how would you know that?"

Aunt Emma shrugged. "I got eyes in my head, and I'm an old woman. There are no new stories out there, only new names for the characters. The two of you had a special kind of chemistry."

"I'd agree with you there, but I'll tell you just how much I loved him. I loved him enough to go away. If I had asked him to follow me, he would have hated life in the city. Eventually, he would have resented me, and we'd have both been miserable. If I had stayed, it would have been me who martyred myself for his dreams. I did the very best for both of us."

"He was heartbroken when you left. Visibly and tragically heartbroken. Some of us feared he'd do something stupid. Turn to drink, or worse."

"I know." Kate raked her fingers over her scalp. "I'm sorry for that. He's a wonderful person. He deserves to be happy, and now he has Pam and the kids. It's the life he always wanted."

"The life he wanted with *you*. Why'd you really come back, dear? Certainly not to visit an old lady like me."

The question shocked Kate. Why *had* she come back? "Convenience." She shrugged. It was a lame reason. Kate tried to dress it up with more words. "I wanted to visit with you, and Joanna told me

Tim was a detective. I knew he'd help me with my internship if I asked."

"Oh now, poo." Aunt Emma smacked her knee. "You were willing to come here and stay with me and your Uncle Owen. No one would willingly spend a summer with that old grump unless they had no other choices. Are you telling me your university couldn't find you an internship with a department that actually had CSI work for you to do?" Aunt Emma crossed her arms over her chest; obviously, she wasn't going to let this drop.

Kate held her tongue.

"Now granted, things have been popping since you've come back to town, but as far as I can remember there has never been a controversial death here. The most the cops get to do is catch a child stealing candy from the grocery, or write a speeding ticket for the out-of-towners, maybe deliver someone home who's had too much to drink. Be truthful. There's more to you being here than convenience sake. And his name is Tim Gibbons —and what's more, I'm not the only one who worked that out. Pam has. I'm sure most of the people in town see it."

"Tim and I were over fifteen years ago. Surely that's long enough that people wouldn't think I have ulterior motives."

"You love him. Tell me you don't, Kate. I have eyes, mind you," Aunt Emma said.

"Yes, I love him. I've always loved him, but it's a sentimental love. A 'wishing him well and happy' kind of love. A friendship. Not a steal-you-away-from-your-family kind of love. And besides..." Kate stopped and focused on her glass of tea.

"Besides what?"

She shrugged. "I wanted a place to be safe and quiet for a little while. I guess that's why I came here. But after all you just said, I'm feeling pretty small and selfish."

"Everyone is selfish once in a while, especially when they're hurting. Doesn't seem like you found what you were looking for here, though."

"How could I? What I want is Ryan back in my life. I want him better. So I came to hide out here for a while to give his doctors a chance to get him stabilized. I thought Scarborough would be a safe distraction."

Aunt Emma patted her hand. "Are you in for the night? I was going to have cobbler and ice cream for dinner."

The discussion behind them, Kate smiled. "That sounds great. I'm going to run up to the gym after we eat, though." Kate checked her watch. "I told Omid I'd meet up with him at 7:30."

"That would be the fire."

"I'm sorry?" Kate looked at her, confused.

"Tim was the fry pan in my metaphor."

69

"And you think I'm after Omid? Seriously? Aunt Emma, I'm married and madly in love with my husband. Omid and I just met. I ran into him at the gas station and mentioned the gym. He happened to be going there tonight, too. I would never ever cheat on Ryan… that's just wrong. No." Kate stood up, thoroughly vexed. "And if you catch anyone gossiping about me, you set everyone straight on all counts, please."

"Easier said than done. You're stirring up more trouble than we've had in a long while. People are looking forward to the fireworks they're anticipating."

"They're going to be disappointed."

"You see that they are."

Kate hit her stride on the treadmill by the time Omid threw his towel over the machine beside her.

"Hey there, I got a head start on you." Kate smiled.

"I see that. I'll have to work to catch up."

"What are you planning for your week off?"

"I got called back on. I need to head to work day after tomorrow."

"Oh?" Kate asked.

"A doctor's wife had their baby earlier than expected." Omid selected his workout on the computer panel.

"Everyone's all right, though?"

"Yes. The baby's family is doing great." He started with a fast walk. "And a few more catfish get a reprieve."

Kate laughed. "I'm glad you're here tonight. I wanted to ask some questions, if you don't mind." Kate lowered her pace so she would have enough breath to talk.

"Are these medical questions or personal?"

"Medical—hospital policy, to be exact."

"Ah. Okay." He pressed a button and began to jog.

"When someone goes into the ER, do they go home with prescriptions filled through the hospital pharmacy?"

"We don't handle that. The doctors write the prescription and the patient gets it filled."

"Could someone steal a prescription pad and use it without a doctor knowing it?"

"Not at our hospital. We don't use prescription pads. We send scripts electronically straight to the pharmacy. That prevents the mistakes made with poor handwriting."

"And you do this on a computer?"

"Hand held devices we carry with us when we're working with the patients. That way we can send it immediately during their consult."

"Could someone get hold of one and send a prescription, as if they were a doctor?"

"I suppose so. Whoever it is would have to be an expert hacker. We have tight security on the devices to prevent such a thing. You're asking these questions because of the children who died?"

"Not specifically. I'm trying to understand if there was a broken link in the chain, allowing bad things to happen that should never have been possible."

"Okay, hypothetically then, the answer is no one could send a fake prescription to the pharmacy by mistake or by premeditation."

"I have another question."

Omid smiled broadly. "It's my turn to ask you a question. Do you have plans tomorrow night? I'm driving to Danville for some Mexican food. I've been craving tacos."

Kate laughed. "Tacos, huh?"

"And I planned to catch a late film."

"What's playing?"

"*Salmon Fishing in Yemen*." His smile crinkled the corners of his eyes. "Please, won't you join me?"

"Thanks, but I'm going hiking tomorrow - get out in nature. My brain feels clogged," Kate said.

"Why's that?"

"Case work. There's been a lot of death this week."

"Yes," Omid agreed, "more than one would expect." A shadow crossed over his face and he offered a tight-lipped smile. "So, you had another question?"

Kate looked up to find Custis glaring at her from across the fitness room. He pointed a threatening finger.

Omid followed her gaze. "Something about that man isn't right," he said.

"Yeah, well, you won't get any argument from me." Kate tapped the red button, and the treadmill came to a stop. She gathered her things to leave.

"Did you walk here tonight?" Omid asked.

"Yes, it's a beautiful night for a walk. I was enjoying the break from the heat. I understand it'll be short lived."

Omid's gaze searched the room until it landed on Custis, who was lifting weights in the mirror, but his attention was focused on them.

Omid stopped his machine. "It's dark outside. I'd feel better if you'd let me drive you home."

Kate glanced at Custis. "Thanks."

Kate's friend Joanna was sitting on the porch swing with a glass of sweet tea in her hand when Kate climbed out of Omid's Jaguar.

"Night, thanks for the ride."

Omid beeped twice and drove off.

"Hey there." Kate went to give Joanna a hug. "I didn't know you'd be in town."

"I came in for Chad's funeral. Stupid idiot boy. God, he's caused a world of hurt. Pemberly's out of her mind. The whole town's in shock. How could this happen, Kate?" Joanna shook her head. "I've never seen anything like it. It's as if everyone turned into a zombie, walking around in a daze. My sister is clinging to her kids like they're drowning. She won't let them get more than three feet from her or she freaks out. I hope Reverend Pines gives a good sermon so people can snap out of this. It's spooky."

"It's hitting close to home for me, too. My students...I don't know how parents can deal with the death of their own child." Kate blew out a breath and looked up at the sky, focusing on the first stars coming out. "My brain is filled with images of my kids. I wonder if they're making good choices and staying safe. Every time my mind turns to home, I panic."

"That's not a good look for an officer of the law."

"CSI intern. But you're right, I have to be professional. I've decided to be a human magnifying glass and focus on the details in front of me."

"Speaking of details in front of you, was that Dr. J. who brought you home?"

"You know him?"

"He treated my mom's goiter. Do you think it's a good idea to be seen tooling around with him?"

"At the moment, I thought it was the best choice I had."

"Why's that?"

"No reason." Kate mumbled and reached over to take a sip of her friend's tea.

"I didn't mean to pry." Joanna pushed off with her foot, making the swing creek as it swayed back and forth.

Kate plopped down on the stair beside her. "Omid has been nothing but a gentleman. He's just being a friend."

"Omid?"

"He's not my doctor. He's just a guy to me."

"A very handsome, well-educated guy. He's also making up for lost time."

Kate swatted away a fly. "I don't understand."

"The Iranian culture prohibits sexual relations outside of marriage. Dr. Javarti never married and…" Joanna offered up a salacious grin. "Well, let's just say he's ruffled the skirts of almost every woman in town under forty, married or unmarried." Joanna winked. "He has an excellent reputation for his fine bedside manner."

Kate wrinkled her nose. "I get your warning, thanks, but it's not an issue." Her phone vibrated on her hip. She pulled her cell from her pocket and read the text message.

Karma bites

Joanna craned her neck to read. "Karma? You posted on Facebook that Ryan's dog's name is Houston."

"I need to call him."

"Yeah, well, it's late. I have to get over to my parent's house. I just wanted to give you a quick hug and tell you I'm around for a few days."

Kate watched as Joanna climbed into her yellow Beetle. She waved until the car was out of sight, and then she called home.

....

EIGHT

Kate smoothed her hand over her new and more appropriate black dress that she had bought the day before. She stood in the back left corner of the church. Tim took up his post on the right. Between the two vantage points, they hoped to cover the congregation. Pemberly stumbled in. It looked like she'd been given a fist full of Valium to get through the ordeal.

The phone buzzed in Kate's bra. She hated to keep it there; it was sweaty and poked at her, but her dress didn't have pockets. She had left her purse in the car to free up her hands. She turned her back to the congregation and fished out her smart phone.

You don't want to stir this pot.

What could Ryan possibly mean? Kate looked at the time stamp. He texted twenty minutes ago. She wondered why the message hadn't been delivered immediately. Probably had to do with whatever Internet site he was using. Kate held up her phone and waggled it at Tim. He responded with two fingers in the air as he mouthed two minutes.

Kate rounded the building, pressing her quick dial for home. The call rang until the answering machine engaged. "Hey, Ryan. It's me. I guess I missed you." Kate said as she walked down the sidewalk into the garden. "I'm trying to figure out what I've done wrong. Did I do something - or not do something – that's upset you?" Kate saw the portly form of Senator Tredegar Orly in the distance, and heard someone yelling angry words at him. "If I did, I'm sorry. I'd like to talk it through with you." Kate sidled up to a tree and peeked around. She saw Custis Scarborough punctuating his diatribe by jabbing a finger at Senator Orly's chest.

Even from this distance, she could tell Custis had whipped himself into full fury. "I'm at a funeral right now, baby. I'll call you later. I love you - never forget that."

Kate pushed the end button as she crept toward the rhododendron bush. She wished she could make out what Custis was saying, but the wind blew the conversation the wrong way. The words that Kate picked out were "uranium," "The hell I will," and "governor." Kate moved closer to see Senator Orly was red-faced and mopping his brow. It seemed to her that the men were about to come to blows. She pressed number three on her phone.

"What have you got?" Tim asked.

"Get to the garden right now. Hurry." Over the phone, she heard the sanctuary door squeak open, then bang. Tim's breath was in the phone.

Seconds later, "I don't see you."

"I'm over by the bushes, but you should...oh, no." Kate leapt forward, sprinting toward the men. Senator Orly had pulled something from his pocket, and then dropped to his knees. As Kate ran the last few steps, Tim's hand was on her back.

Senator Orly fumbled with a prescription vial. Kate knelt beside him and took it from his hand. Nitroglycerin.

She popped the top and tipped a pill into the senator's open palm. He slipped the pill under his tongue, fell down on his hip, before rolling onto his back. Tim was on the phone with dispatch, getting an ambulance en route. Custis stood with his arms folded across his chest, a smirk on his face.

"Katie, I need you to go up to the parking lot and show the EMTs where we are. Tell them stat."

"Do you have anything in the squad car that would help?" Kate asked.

"Not for this I don't."

Kate took off at a run. She could already hear the sirens wailing on the other side of town.

It took the whole crew, Tim, and several men recruited from the sanctuary to get Senator Orly up the garden hill to the ambulance. Senator Orly had the reputation for being a lifelong lover of fried chicken, potato salad, and pork barbeque. He must tip the scale at over four hundred pounds.

Custis was not one of the men helping with the lifting. He had wandered off long before help arrived, Kate noticed. While the men made the climb, Kate returned to the garden. Scanning the ground, she picked up her discarded phone and Senator Orly's medications. She squatted down and put her ear to the ground. She hoped from the new vantage point she would see something she'd missed. Something to tell her what Custis had been going on about.

Tim came back to find her fanny up.

Kate jumped to her feet, brushing the grass from her knees. "How does he look?"

"We'll have to wait and see. What've you got there?"

She held out the Nitro bottle.

"Spit it out," Tim said.

"Spit what out?"

"You've got a theory."

"I don't. And even if I did, it would be unprofessional to have a theory, so I wouldn't tell you."

They started up the path. "But you've got one."

"Not so much a theory as a concern."

Tim's fingers rested on Kate's lower back as he guided her up the stairs. "Go on."

"Two heart attacks in two weeks. Both men on Nitro pills."

"Most of the men in town over a certain age have them, I'd imagine," Tim said.

"Nitro is for angina, so I don't think so. I'm wondering if we could send this to the lab and maybe my uncle's pills, too. See if they are what the label says they are. Senator Orly didn't seem to respond to his pill."

Tim stopped and touched Kate's elbow so she'd turn to face him. "All right. After the funeral, we'll go get your Uncle Owen's pills. Realize though, neither man was healthy. Senator Orly's been a heart attack waiting to happen for over a decade now. This is probably a wild goose chase, but I'm willing to scratch this idea off your list. I don't want it rumbling in the background. We need to stay focused."

I, Owen Jenkins, being about as sound in mind and body as I ever have been in my adult life, do declare this my last will and testament. Whatever I've got at the time the Good Lord calls me home is to be split equally between my wife, Emma Sue Jenkins, and my niece, Katherine Sophia Hamilton (Kate). My niece, though, is the one who should make all the decisions. My wife has got to be off her rocker, or she wouldn't have put up with the likes of me for the last fifty some-odd years. Kate shows much more sense by keeping her distance. So now, Kate has to step up and watch out for my Em.

One stipulation, though. Kate is not to sell my great granddaddy's land. Not split it up. Not rent it, lease it, nothing. Not to anyone, under any circumstances. It stays in the family, period. The next in line are Kate's cousins on Emma's side. Kate can pick one of them to be in her will. Kate, make sure that you stipulate that this land is never ever to be sold no matter how many millions they offer for it. This land is not for sale.

Other than that, I don't care much what you girls do.

Signed before God and my lawyer,

Owen Jefferson Jenkins IV

"What's all this about?" Kate asked.

Neil Oliver, Uncle Owen's lawyer, took off his glasses and rubbed them with his linen handkerchief. "Your uncle insisted on writing his own will. He thought the language that I might incorporate would give folks an opportunity to trick or cheat you into comcompromising the family land."

"It sounds like this has something to do with Scarborough Mining. Aunt Emma said they wanted to put a holding pond on Jenkins Hillock."

"Yes, well, you're right." Neil Oliver rested his elbows on the arms of his chair, steepled his fingers, and thrust the points under his chin. Kate watched him gather his thoughts.

"The Village of Scarborough is at odds," Neil began. "There are two camps: one camp says progress and economics, the other says tradition and environment. Your uncle lived in the second camp. And he had more power than most when it came to allowing or disallowing Scarborough Mining to fulfill its dreams of mega-wealth. We're talking billions with a capital 'B', Kate."

Kate scooted to the edge of her chair.

"You see, the topography of the area puts almost the entire vein of uranium under Scarborough Knoll. A smaller vein does run through Jenkins Hillock, but that vein wouldn't be profitable to mine. There's not enough raw product. But your uncle's property does have an important role to play in the uranium production. It is somewhat of an obstacle, actually. Scarborough Mining would be required to set up a containment pond, placed to protect the contents from any effect of flooding, should a flood like the one Noah faced ever descend upon us. If the river was to flood as far as Scarborough Knoll, which is impossible to imagine, it could create a radioactive catastrophe in the Roanoke River."

"Why can't they use Pemberly's land?" Kate asked.

"Oh, they did studies. The Wilks family was very keen on renting their land to Scarborough Mining; in fact, Mrs. Wilks was one of the first investors in the mining company and sits on their board. But their land is too low. It would have to be Jenkins Hillock, or they can't move forward. Not that they can move forward at this time anyway, though many are hopeful about the upcoming legislative session."

Kate heaved a breath. "Ah. The holding pond must be the unfinished business Custis Scarborough wanted to talk to me about."

Aunt Emma tilted her head to the side. "You looked relieved, dear."

"I was afraid he wanted to rehash the time I testified against him," Kate said. "Mr. Oliver, is there anything you need from either my Aunt Emma or me?"

"Not at the moment. There's a series of steps to navigate through. Do you and Mrs. Jenkins wish to continue with me as lawyer, or do you prefer to seek counsel in Boston?"

"For now, we'll carry on with you, Neil, if that's all right," Aunt Emma said. "You know all of our business, and there's no reason for a change." She gathered her purse, and stood to shake hands with him.

"Thank you, Emma. I'll keep you and Kate updated on how things progress with probate."

As they moved from the icebox-cold office out onto the sweltering street, Kate pulled the sweater from around her shoulders. Aunt Emma seemed not to mind the heat at all.

"Did you hear my stomach growling in there?" Aunt Emma whispered from behind her hand. "I was so embarrassed. I need something to eat. How about you?" She pointed down the street to Country Kitchen.

It looked too far to walk on such a hot day and too close to drive, but ever since Kate had seen Custis yelling at Senator Orly, she had some questions she wanted to run by her aunt.

The bell jingled brightly as they went in. The apple-cheeked cashier stood behind the register. After ordering sweet tea and egg salad sandwiches, they moved to the two-top tucked in the far corner.

"Aunt Emma, do you know anything about Pemberly and her husband's breakup?" Kate asked.

"Well, I do and I don't. I can tell you what the gossips are saying. How true any of it is, I can't say for sure. It's more to do with that blasted Scarborough Mining."

"Was he pro-mining, too?"

"Oh, he was very much pro-mining. The problem was that American Mine Works offered to buy out Pemberly's shares in Scarborough Mining. It was a good offer by all accounts. Many of the other investors have already sold their shares to them. The Wilks family would have made a tidy profit, but not the hundreds of millions that Pemberly is anticipating. She believes those millions are close at hand because of the upcoming vote. Her husband thinks the vote will fail again, especially with Tredegar Orly standing so staunchly against it. Jason Wilks wanted Pemberly to take the deal. The fiasco turned into a drunken fight at the country club. Pemberly threw her mint julep in his face." Aunt Emma leaned out of the way to let the waitress put their plates down. "Thank you, dear. That looks lovely."

When she and Kate were alone again, Aunt Emma continued. "Afterward, he hightailed it back to Charlotte, where he took a job in finance and hasn't been back to Scarborough since."

"But there's more to this than getting the bill through the legislature. I read that the governor swore he'd veto it if it crossed his desk."

"Owen said that's politics. The man needed to watch how he was viewed in Northern Virginia. He couldn't win a gubernatorial election without a good number of those folks. He probably said what needed to be said. Can you imagine the tax dollars he'd be turning down? He'll sign it in the end. At least, that's what Owen believed."

"Aunt Emma, why would Senator Orly's vote be so significant?"

"With age comes privilege. Tredegar Orly has served in the state senate for nigh on forty years. Since this is his hometown, folks would respect his vote and follow along. Have you heard anything about how he's doing?"

"Last I heard, he was in critical condition, and the doctors were doing what they could. Tim said Omid is his doctor."

"There's a blessing. Dr. Javarti is a professor, so he'll know the very newest and best things to do."

"Wasn't Omid Uncle Owen's physician, too?"

"Owen saw a man up at the VA in Richmond. We'd drive up there every few months for them to take a look-see at how your uncle was getting along. He drove Owen batty with his lectures on nutrition and exercise, tried to get him to stop smoking, if you can imagine such a thing. I tried to switch Owen to turkey bacon once. You never heard such a commotion. Nope, nothing changed Owen. Not a blessed thing."

Kate and Emma quietly ate their sandwiches, each focused inwardly.

"Aunt Emma, did American Mine Works ever offer Uncle Owen any money for Jenkins Hillock?"

"Why yes, I believe that's what brought on your uncle's heart attack. The ladies from my Bible study group had come for tea. We heard Owen in his office blustering away, then it sounded like he was in pain, and I rushed in. I found him there on the floor, the receiver still in his hand. I put a Nitro pill under his tongue, and Rose called 9-1-1. The paramedics collected him and took him up to the hospital. Dr. Javarti said while they were racing the gurney to the ICU, Owen slipped away from them."

"You miss Uncle Owen, don't you?"

"I do. He's been part of my life since I was six-years-old. Feels like I lost an arm and a leg. But there's also a certain amount of peace. He's in a better place now, and all the torment he lived with is over."

Kate fiddled with her straw wrapper. "Did he ever talk about what happened in Vietnam?"

"Never. Kept it all bottled up inside. Has Ryan ever talked to you about what happened to him in Afghanistan?"

"No, ma'am. But his buddy Zack read the reports, and he told me. Knowing what happened, I can understand Ryan's brain's reaction. Nobody should be able to live through a day like that and walk away unchanged. A normal human being shouldn't be able to see what Ryan saw, lose the number of brothers he lost, and go on his merry way. Now that would truly be sick."

"That's exactly how I felt about Owen."

Kate's phone buzzed, and she glanced at the caller ID. She excused herself and did a half-turn before answering. "It's my day off."

Tim cleared his throat. "I thought you should know. Tredegar Orly just died."

NINE

....

"I'm walking this up to the post office; you want to keep me company?" Tim asked.

Kate stood on the first stair going up to the station house and wasn't really in the mood to walk in the heat, but she found herself saying yes anyway.

They had gone about a half-block when Kate asked, "Seven deaths in just over two weeks. Okay, is it me or is this pretty strange?"

Tim grinned. "I'm blaming you."

"How so?" She tilted her head in confusion.

"You came to town and suddenly we have no room at the funeral home for any more bodies. You might be the Angel of Death."

Kate smacked his arm.

"It's wrong for me to say this," Tim said, "but those floods in the Midwest are well timed."

"How does the Mississippi River have anything to do with this?"

"Four small town white kids - and that's not me being racial, it's just me stating the truth - dead within a week from an overdose? It just doesn't happen. If this were a slow news cycle, we wouldn't be able to move for all of the reporters that would be swarming us. Right now, everyone is focused on the folks who truly need the exposure and help."

"I've seen a few reporters at the funerals."

"Right," Tim said. "But they're Virginia reporters. It hasn't spread like smallpox to the national news cycle. If we got thronged by them, it would make everything that much more complicated."

"And it's complicated enough. What do Pemberly and Wayne have in common? Wayne isn't Virginia blue blood, so they don't move in the same social circles. He doesn't have anywhere near her money. They're a generation apart. They were on opposite sides of the uranium deal. There must be some other connection, though." Kate had to stretch her legs to keep stride with Tim.

"I'll see if I can dig anything up today when I interview the drug store employees."

"While you're at it, you should drag Custis Scarborough's sorry ass in and ask him a thing or two."

"Katherine Hamilton, did you cuss? What are you learning up there in Boston?"

"Excuse me, his sorry behind. He was furious with Senator Orly, red-faced and spitting when he yelled at the senator. If it weren't for the wind, I'd know what brought on Orly's heart attack."

"They were fighting about what they always fight about. Tredegar wanted to protect the river, and Custis wants to be a billionaire."

"Still, there might be something there that would help. If you asked me to lay money on an outcome, I'd lay it on Custis' head. He's the only psychopath I know."

"Psychopath, huh? How'd you come to that conclusion?"

"He's anti-social. He hates people, unless, of course, they're serving his purposes, and then he'll charm the pants off them. And he's bright, but shiftless. What does he do for a living exactly?"

"He's listed as the CEO of Scarborough Mining, which means he gets a paycheck from their investors, but there's probably not a lot for him to do day-in and day-out. He's got time on his hands. But I wouldn't say shiftless. He does have a law degree from the College of William and Mary. They don't exactly hand those out."

"True. But summer of our sophomore year - the fertilizer factory. Arson is a big flashing neon sign for psychopaths and serial killers, especially an arson that was that spectacular."

"Thanks to your eyewitness testimony, he spent three years in juvie. You'd think their psychiatrists would have flagged his file."

"Have you seen his file?"

"No, and I won't, because it was sealed when he turned eighteen. Go back to 'charms the pants off people.' Custis ever do that to you?"

Kate stilled. "You know the answer to that. You and I were together all through high school. But I will tell you who he was doing it with: Doris Arthur, and she still has the hots for Custis."

"Says who? You weren't around for the last fifteen years."

"Says my Aunt Emma, who saw his hands up her skirt at the country club last month. She keeps me up on all the scuttlebutt."

"Sounds like you have a story line forming in your head, and that's just bad detective work. I've told you this."

She kicked at the gravel. "I'm not here to play detective. I'm a CSI intern, here to help gather evidence at crime scenes and process it for use in supporting possible trial cases."

"So all of these insights you've been sharing since you've come back into town…"

"That's just me running my mouth—feel free to ignore me."

"As if that were possible."

They walked along without a word. Tim went into the Post Office, and then they turned back to the station. Kate took in the number of empty storefronts. The shops that were open looked run down in the heel. Clean, but well worn.

"Nothing in on the tox report for the teens?" Kate asked.

"Nothing yet." Tim shoved his hands in his pockets. "The lab understands there's the possibility of an ongoing risk, so our reports got bumped to the top of the list. I'm expecting them sooner rather than later. The preliminary ME report says that all the kids died of respiratory distress."

"As did Wayne."

"I have nothing on him yet." Tim returned a wave from a couple across the street.

"How long for the feedback on the Nitroglycerin?"

"I can't say. It all depends on how we show up in the queue. Tredegar Orly's name on the file pushes it up on the list."

"It isn't supposed to work this way. I mean, in the movies those reports turn around in a few hours, a day at most."

"Welcome to the head-banging-into-a-wall reality of police work."

"When I'm studying this in the classroom, we learned that it takes x amount of time to process. It feels very different than this. It's so frustrating. Have you thought about getting a judge to order a shutdown of the pharmacy?"

"I don't have any evidence to suggest that to him, but I did talk to Doris. She's gone back, pulled the names of everyone on Nitroglycerin, and is swapping out their meds. That's what she's doing today."

"Is she bringing the old prescriptions back for analysis? Shouldn't an officer be with her, or shouldn't I be with her, for that matter, so the medications can be properly gathered as evidence?"

"Do you think Doris has committed a crime here, Kate?"

Kate stopped and stared at Tim. "If two men died because of issues surrounding their medications, culpability should be assigned. This has to lead to something more sinister."

"Are you always this paranoid?" He tapped her on the back to get her walking again. "Right now, we have two heart patients who died. I'm betting the medication composition reports come up normal. I'm really only having the analysis done on the off chance you're right."

"You're placating me?" Kate's voice jumped an octave. "So *no* to the officer following Doris around. And no to her collecting the evidence properly. No to a proper chain of custody."

"That's right. The answer is *no*. No proof that there's a problem. No other person who's even questioning events. There's *no* way I can move forward with this until I get lab results. Remember, in order to collect the medication as evidence, I'd need a warrant. And *no,* I have nothing to present to the judge other than, 'Katie has a hunch.'" He said the last words with air quotes.

"You could do the collection, if folks were willing."

"No, I couldn't, because of HIPPA. Now drop it." Tim sounded more than a little exasperated. "I have to figure out how the old Oxycodone formula got through the cracks and into the hands of Pemberly and Wayne. Let's not make this bigger than it is. Now, when I interview the drug store employees, you can't be in the room with me, but you can watch the feed with the other officers. Just keep your mouth shut, so the officers can focus on their body language."

"Is Doris Arthur going to be answering more questions?"

"Yes, but not today."

"Can I be there?"

"It's best if you're not, Katie." His tone softened.

"Seriously? Why not?"

"The Arthurs are a tight knit family. They tend to huddle up when they feel one of their own is under attack."

"I'm not attacking Doris. I just want to hear her answers."

Tim shuffled his feet. "It's not about the pharmacy. She's Pam's cousin."

"Huh? Oh…" Kate walked a few paces, processing that information. "Am I creating grief in your family, Tim? I don't mean to."

"I never thought you did," Tim said. "Pam is very insecure, that's all. She'll get over it."

"Once I leave."

"Yup. Pretty much."

"So why'd you say yes to me when I asked for an internship with you if you knew that I'd be making waves?"

They stood outside of the front door of the police station. Tim turned to face Kate. "You've always made waves in my marriage. Pam was around when you and I were together, and she compares our marriage to what I had with you. I agreed to your coming down because I thought if Pam saw us interacting professionally, she'd give it a rest. Seems it's got her more riled up than before, though. She says she can tell that…" Tim scrubbed a hand over his head. "I also agreed because you sounded like you were in a bad place. You'd have to be, if you were willing to live a whole summer with your Uncle Owen. I told you a long time ago, Katydid, I'd always be there for you. And I meant it."

Kate pushed a strand of hair behind her ear. "Am I hurting you? Should I leave?"

Tim pushed the door open. "No, to both questions."

Standing behind the two-way mirror, Kate observed Tim questioning the woman. "Ma'am, on that date, you are listed as being scheduled to work, but you're saying you weren't there. You took your child to the doctor. Did you find someone to cover your shift that day?"

Betty Sue Ridgeway caved her shoulders in as if she were trying to fold herself into something smaller. "Yes, sir. Cal Simpson took over for me."

"I don't have Cal on my employee roster."

"Cal doesn't work at the pharmacy anymore since he made all that money with the online gambling," Betty Sue explained. "He quit to stay home with his daughter."

Tim wrote down a few notes. "That's my last question for today. Thank you for your time and cooperation."

Tim walked into the viewing room where Kate sat next to the other two officers. "Mandrel, do you know anyone named Cal Simpson?"

"Sure," Officer Mandrel said. "The Simpsons go to my church. They've been on the prayer list for months."

"Why? What's going on with their family?" Tim pulled a metal chair over and sat down.

"During the ice storm their daughter, Anna, was in a car accident. The dad worked at the pharmacy, the mom quit her job cleaning houses to take care of Anna. The girl's a paraplegic now, and they don't have any medical insurance. Their house was approaching foreclosure. It was a big mess. Then about two weeks ago, Cal came to church and thanked everyone for their prayers. He said God had blessed his family with respite from their financial crisis, though they still needed prayers for the recuperation of their daughter, but his financial issues were over. It was a joyful thing for our congregation."

"I'm sure it was," Kate said.

Tim scraped his chair against the terrazzo flooring. "I'm heading over to Cal's place to see if he'll come in for a chat." He pointed at Kate. "Do you want to ride with me? Or do you want to take off for the day?"

"No, I'll come with you."

The woman stood at the front door with her eyes opened too widely. She blanched and staggered.

Kate grabbed the woman by the shoulders and helped her to the sofa. Sitting beside Mrs. Simpson, Kate reached for her hand. "Can Detective Gibbons fetch you a glass of water, ma'am?"

Mrs. Simpson raised her head. "Just tell me quick. Is he dead? How'd it happen?"

Tim crouched by the woman's side. "Oh, no, ma'am. I'm so sorry. Probably the last time an officer showed up at your door, they came to tell you about your daughter's accident."

Mrs. Simpson nodded.

"No, ma'am. We came by to ask Cal a few questions about his time working in the pharmacy, that's all."

Mrs. Simpson took a minute to recover. Her face turned bright red, and she fanned herself with her hand. When she seemed to have regained her equilibrium, Tim asked, "What time are you expecting your husband back, ma'am?"

"He went fishing this morning, said he'd be back by lunch, but here it is dinnertime." A buzzer sounded from upstairs. "That's my daughter. I have to go check on her." She pushed herself up. "I'll be right back."

While she was gone, Tim looked around the room.

"Everything looks new," Kate said. "Smells new, too - carpet and paint."

Tim looked like he was chewing something over, so Kate sat quietly and let him process.

Mrs. Simpson walked back into the room. "She's fine. She wondered what was going on down here."

"Ma'am, what kind of car does your husband drive?"

"He has a Ford 150 pickup, brand new this week." Mrs. Simpson smiled.

Tim walked to the window and pushed the lace curtains aside. "Looks like you have a new van, too."

"Yes, we needed one to accommodate Anna's wheelchair when we take her to her therapy."

"Does the insurance cover that?" Tim asked. "Oh, no. We don't have any insurance. It would be wonderful if we did. My daughter's accident has been very costly."

"It seems you're coming through okay." Tim moved back into the room. "The pharmacy said that Cal quit."

"Yes, he did, to help with Anna." Mrs. Simpson pointed at the ceiling to indicate her daughter upstairs. "And I'm so grateful. She's a teen and too heavy for me."

"How was he able to afford to do that, ma'am?"

A big grin swept across Mrs. Simpson's face. "He won the money off the gambling sites." Sudden concern filled her eyes. "I hope that's okay. Cal told me it was legal."

"He won a lot of money, then?" Tim tilted his head. "Oh yes, enough to pay off Anna's bills, do some repairs around the house. And we have enough put aside to get us through retirement."

"Is he still gambling?" Tim asked.

Kate wrapped her hands around her knees and held her tongue.

"No, no. I asked him to stop," Mrs. Simpson explained. "Gambling can be addictive and after what we've been through – it's enough. No, we prayed for a miracle, and God gave us the right playing cards, and then Cal stopped. We have everything we asked for, except, of course, Anna being able to walk. But we're sure with prayer and hard work that will come, too."

"He went fishing today?"

"Yes, up at his favorite spot near Scarborough Knoll. He and Custis fished it since they were boys together in Sunday school."

"Thank you, ma'am. We'll stop in another time to talk to Cal."

Tim worked his jaw as they walked toward the squad car.

"What?" Kate asked.

"It feels like we're about to hit a dead end."

TEN

....

The beep-beep startled Kate from her thoughts; she turned her head to glance over her shoulder. She smiled and waved as Omid pulled up beside her.

"Can I give you a lift? You look like you're melting in that black shirt."

Kate made her way around and let herself into the Jag. She was grateful for the air conditioning.

"Hey, there," she said.

"I'm on my way to pick up one of Maggie May's boxed meals," Omid said as he drove down Main Street. "I'm heading to the old train trestle to watch the sunset. Want to come? Looks like you have too many emotions brewing to be comfortable inside. Big emotions take space and fresh air."

"I do have a lot on my mind. A picnic sounds nice. I was hoping to run into you, anyway. I have some questions about who has access to medical records and how they're stored."

Omid pulled over to the curb. "Glad to help. Why don't you stay in the air conditioning while I run in?"

The spot Omid chose was picturesque and serene. The river bubbled twenty feet below their dangling feet. The sun's last rays licked over the surface, making the water glitter. Fireflies flickered from the shoreline.

Dinner had been simple and delicious. No one made homemade bread like Maggie May. She deserved her reputation as the best cook in the county.

"Did you have enough to eat?" Omid asked.

Kate groaned in reply. "Too much. It was too good to stop. 'Fat as a tick.' Do you know that expression?"

Omid chuckled and reached out to tuck a stray curl behind her ear. "You could never be fat, or anything but beautiful." He lowered his lips to hers.

"Oh," Kate gasped, leaning away. "Oh, dear. No. Omid, I'm sorry if I gave you the wrong impression." She wiped her mouth with her napkin. "I'm here only as a friend."

Omid rubbed the back of his neck. "It's me who must apologize. I read the signs incorrectly. Forgive me."

"I'm married. I thought you knew."

"I heard this, yes. But you left him. And you're no longer wearing your wedding ring. I obviously made assumptions... jumped to conclusions..."

"I'm wearing my wedding ring, see?" Kate held up her left index finger with the thick platinum band engraved with Celtic knots. "It's my husband's wedding band, though. And he's wearing mine on his pinky." Kate twisted the ring around and around. "When I left Boston, we both needed a reminder of the other person's commitment. We both understood our own. So we exchanged each other's rings."

"Why didn't you do your internship in Boston and stay with your husband?"

"He's not well." She rounded her shoulders, caving inward. "He's home from the war. PTSD. He has violent episodes with dissociative reactions, and he's hurt me because of it - not badly, just bruises. But it scared him. I was afraid he might become suicidal if he thought it would protect me."

"How's he doing now that you're out of the picture?"

Kate breathed in deeply, letting her gaze follow the graceful descent of a blue heron, landing on the sandy shore below. "He says he's making progress."

"But you don't believe that."

"It's going to take a long time to heal. I want him to learn to feel safe enough that I can come home. I miss him terribly." Kate reached out to gather their wrappings and stuff them back in the cardboard carton. "It's this feeling of missing him that's worse than when he was in Afghanistan. I have him back physically, but not mentally. I'm going to have to adjust to being married to a new Ryan."

"This must be very difficult for you, Kate. And on top of everything, you came to Scarborough even though you hate it here," Omid observed.

"I don't hate it," Kate said. "I just don't fit."

"I know the feeling. When I'm in the U.S., I dream of Karaj. When I'm in Karaj, I dream of…"

"Catfish."

"Exactly." Omid chuckled.

Bad Boys played over Kate's phone; she leaned back so she could drag it from her hip pocket. Tim.

"Kate, you've got to get up to the Knoll. I need your CSI expertise."

Fear gripped her throat as she tried to speak. "Is it Cal?"

"I found him floating in the water."

JLILIL
ꓶꓶꓶꓶ

Kate moved carefully down the embankment well away from the taped off area. Tim had sent a cruiser to collect her. Kate had asked the officer to take her by her house for her waders, in case she needed to take pictures of the shoreline. The waders were in her backpack on her back, restricting her arm movements as she held onto the branches, and then made a final leap to the water's edge.

Mosquitoes whined through the air. Kate had doused herself with SkinSoSoft, hoping to keep the worst of them at bay. The high humidity made her skin tacky and gnats swarmed her. She gazed up the river, hoping a breeze would accumulate over the water and whisk them all away. It was wishful thinking. Tonight, the air was still as if the Knoll was holding its breath, waiting. The land, though, was a different story. All about her, the woods came alive. As the evening songs of the birds died down, the tree frogs and crickets filled in the empty spaces, growing their discordant notes into a full country-evening symphony. Deepening indigo painted the sky; the first stars offered tentative twinkles.

The police department had set up massive LED lights, making the taped area as bright as daytime. A command tent was set up. The ambulance slowly pulled its way up the slope toward the dirt road. The flashing lights were off. That was confirmation enough that Cal was dead. A hearse moved into the vacated spot.

Kate's thoughts went back to Cal's wife. Mrs. Simpson had been sure they were there to tell her bad news. Premonition? Conditioning from her daughter's recent accident? Or did she believe Cal was in danger? Maybe his death wasn't an accident.

Kate raised her hand in the air, a childhood trick she remembered. The gnats were supposed to swarm the highest point of your body. It hadn't worked for her then, and it sure wasn't working now - at keeping the pests away, that is. It did catch Tim's attention.

He moved toward her, answering questions and re-directing his men as he wended his way. "Good. You're here."

"Yup, put me to work. What have you found?"

"About a case of empty beer bottles. Looks like Cal got drunk, tripped, and drowned."

"Looks like?" Kate asked, slapping at the mosquito that landed on his cheek. He ducked before her hand landed.

"Henry said you got your waders. Put 'em on and follow me."

Rubber encased up to her chest, Kate grabbed hold of the rope someone had tied to a tree and used it to move hand-over-hand down into the water. Here the current was manageable, but Tim reached for her hand to keep her steady. They moved further out into the water, and then Tim turned and pointed toward the shore. "What do you see?"

Kate took a deep breath and stared at the shore.

"Don't over think this; just tell me what you see."

"There's a log where people would lean for comfort under the overhang of the tree that would keep the sun off. There are a lot of beer bottles. They all look to have the same label and they're stacked in a pile. I'd assume they're recent since the label isn't sun faded or peeling off. I can make out the box they came in. There are two footprints in the mud, but it comes from the slope, not from the log. Long steps, like someone was running."

"Those are my footprints," Tim said. "I saw the body facedown in the water and ran over, hoping I had caught him in time. But he had been dead for a while. This heat makes quick work of decomposition."

"I'm confused. From where the fishing tackle is lying surely there should have been some other footprints."

"Should have been."

"And why is it muddy? It hasn't rained since I've been here."

"Good question. If I were a betting man, I'd say someone used that bucket over there and threw some water on the ground to hide evidence."

"Not an accident, then." Kate lost her balance and wriggled to keep upright. Tim reached around, grabbed her waist, and pulled her to him. He was solid.

"I'm a detective. I don't come to any conclusions until all of the pieces are put together. Right now, there are a bunch of missing pieces."

Kate pushed away from Tim, but kept a tight grip on his hand.

Tim gestured with his free hand. "We need all this carefully photographed from out here, before I put up the number cones. We'll leave footprints when we do."

They moved together towards the shoreline, away from the crime scene tape.

"How'd you get his body out of here?" Kate asked.

"I did the initial photographs, and then we put him on a backboard and floated him down to where you found the ropes tied. I wanted to keep the area as intact as possible."

"Did you already tell his wife?"

"Our chaplain does our notifications. She's already braced for it."

"That was my feeling. You might want to get hold of Cal's computer to see about his poker history."

"The warrants came in while you were taking your dinner break. A unit already went by and picked it up."

"Do you think Anna's accident wasn't an accident?"

"Doubtful. She was driving in an ice storm. The girl in front with her died at the scene. The girl in the back told the cops what happened, and she walked out of there without a scratch. Hard to stage something like that. Are you a conspiracy theorist?" "No, why?"

"Just seems to be your mindset. You used to be inquisitive and now you seem…"

"Paranoid? There is something odd happening. And I think when you've got all the data, it's all going to boil down to one psychopath. Custis Scarborough."

Tim chuckled. "That's what he said you'd say."

"You talked to him?"

"Yup. I wondered if he'd had a hair of the dog down here with Cal, or if he had seen Cal at all today. He said no, and his maid said she had brought his lunch to his room and woke him up. His dad said they had an argument about his drinking, and his mom said she didn't want any of the emergency vehicles messing up her lawn."

"So no one without a vested interest in keeping Custis from going back to jail saw him today? Look over here. There's a beer bottle tucked behind this log." Kate snapped pictures from various angles.

"Myopia is a bad trait for a detective," Tim said.

As she used her pen to lift the brown bottle from the dried leaves, some beer spilled out onto her hand. "Here's a bad trait for a beer – it's blue."

Tim stared down at the liquid on her glove.

"I'd have the ME run a tox report on Cal to check for Rohypnol poisoning," Kate said. "I think he was roofied."

"And the beers over there?"

"I'll bet you my next paycheck that not a one of them has a fingerprint. I'd say that site was staged. But you're the detective. I collect and process crime scenes."

"You work for free, so that's not much of a bet." Tim helped her climb the bank, so she could keep the bottle steady on her pen. "You've got the wrong calling. You should reconsider."

"Teaching? I wouldn't give it up, but why do you say that?"

"I had a bunch of reports sitting on my desk when I came in. The teens found at Pemberly's house both had the same results: Oxycodone overdoses. The powdered residue is from the old formulation, and the kids shouldn't have had access to it. Also, Wayne Brody died of respiratory failure attributed to the use of high dosage of Oxycodone with a pre-existing asthmatic condition. I don't have anything on the twins yet. I'm hoping that'll come in to-morrow."

"Okay. So there's negligence involved."

"I have more," Tim said. "The Nitroglycerin tablets were placebo pills - sugar."

"All of the pills from the pharmacy, or just the pills for Uncle Owen?" They made their way to the CSI van.

"Your uncle and Senator Orly had placebo pills and the other pills Doris picked up were legitimate," Tim said.

"Why would anyone do that? Nitroglycerin helps people with angina. Angina isn't a heart attack; it just feels like a heart attack. They take a pill, wait five minutes, and then take another one. If they're still in pain, they know it's an MI and to call for help."

"MI? Lay terms, please."

"A myocardial infarction. Heart attack. So if someone gave Uncle Owen and Senator Orly placebo pills, all that would do is make my uncle or the senator *think* they were having an MI. Wheth-er they were or not, they'd go to the hospital. The hospital would confirm the heart attack or see that it was angina..." Kate's eyes were unfocused as she concentrated on this newest twist. She turned suddenly to catch Tim's eye. "Doesn't that sound weird to you? And everyone else in town got the real deal? Huh. "

"We can't place blame with Doris straight out. Someone could have switched the pills that Orly and Owen had at any point after they left the drug store. Making a connection directly to the drugstore would be difficult." Tim opened the back door of the CSI van and pulled out a collection bag. He bent over to fill in the information.

"For the placebo pills maybe, but not for the Oxycodone. It has the name on the label."

"Yup, looks like we've got us a mess."

Kate went home, but sleep eluded her. What did she know? Eight people who shouldn't be dead were dead in a matter of weeks. Only five were intended: Pemberly, Orly, Owen, Wayne, and Cal. The teens were mistakes. And Pemberly was alive. Somebody had been switching meds. Somebody had been giving folks meds they shouldn't have, and they seemed to be generated at the pharmacy. Cal had worked in the pharmacy, and he had suddenly come into a boatload of money. The day they started to question the pharmacy staff, he shows up drowned. How convenient was that? Not so much for his family, or for the police solving the case, but very convenient for the mastermind behind all the murders. Was any of this random?

Sure, Uncle Owen was a terrible person and not a soul liked him, but would someone want him dead? Tredegar Orly was well liked. His funeral was huge. Not a dry eye in the place. Pemberly was a country-club-going, tennis-playing, garden-partier. Her husband had left her. But he had been in North Carolina, surely someone would recognize him if he had come to town prior to Chad's funeral. Around and around Kate's mind went until she was dizzy.

Little girls who play with fire get burned. I smell smoke.

"Baby, I'm scared," Kate said to Ryan after he answered her call.

Ryan sounded groggy as if he was just waking up. "What's going on?"

"Why did you send me that text?"

"I can't text you, Kate. I refuse to use cell phones. You know that. What text did you get?"

"You haven't sent me texts over the Internet?" Kate's voice warbled.

"I didn't even know that was possible. What did they say?"

"Um. Random things. They didn't make a whole lot of sense. If you're not sending them, then who is? Do you know how I could find out?"

"Zack's here. He can figure this out. Hang on."

Kate chewed off three fingernails before she heard, "Hey, sweet girl."

"Hey, Zack. I'm a little wigged out."

"That's what Ryan's saying."

"Now that I know these texts aren't from Ryan, I'm scrolling back. They look kind of threatening."

" What did your boss say? Tim, isn't it?"

"Yes, Tim. I didn't show him. I thought Ryan had sent them until just now. So when I read them that way, the texts don't sound menacing, just kind of…off."

"Do you have access to your computer?"

"Yes, my laptop." Kate moved over to her bedside table and pushed the on button to boot up.

"Good, I want you to plug your phone in. I'm e-mailing you a web link that will let me go in and take a look around. You'll want to take any nudie pictures you sent to Ryan out of your photo album. I don't need that in my head."

"It's all PG, I promise. Your email just came through. I'm all hooked up. Should I press 'accept'? You don't think Ryan did this and forgot or…"

"He couldn't have, sweetheart. He's at the VA during the day, and I'm with him at night. And besides, he threw his laptop out the upstairs window, so it's a fallen soldier."

╪╫╫╫

Tim looked up from his desk. "Why are you here?"

Kate walked in and set a Styrofoam cup of black coffee in front of him. "I couldn't sleep."

"Occupational hazard."

"Good thing I'm a school teacher. It occurred to me last night that Pemberly might be in danger. And she's also probably the only person who could tell us whether she picked up her prescription from Cal."

"It occurred to me, too. She's safe for now. She's in Roanoke in the mental hospital on suicide watch. Her husband took her down there yesterday and signed her in."

"The whole story, please?" Kate blew on the surface of her own coffee.

"We knew she was taking Nardil for depression. But how she ended up on suicide watch? That I don't know."

"Her husband does. From what Aunt Emma says, he's a narcissist. I bet he'd answer your questions just for the attention."

"I tried. He said he's not interested. He said he has no information, and it's not in his best interest to talk to us about anything that might further incriminate his wife."

"Well, that's you. What about a reporter? I've been reading along in the Scarborough Sun and their reporter, Eva Mason, seems sharp. What if we made a list of questions, and she went and interviewed him about his family's tragedy? She could play the sympathetic role. It would give him an opportunity to lay out the story he wants known, and there might be a thread of truth in it. She could get him on tape. A narcissist would eat this like pudding." Kate moved towards the only empty seat in Tim's office.

"No 'g,'" he said.

"What?"

"You've been up north too long. You say all of the 'ings' now. 'A narcissist would eat this like puddin'.'"

Kate rolled her eyes. But noticed he was looking up Eva Mason's phone number as he said it.

ELEVEN

S weetheart, you need to head out of town," Zack said.

Kate's hand trembled as she held the phone to her ear. "Is Ryan okay?"

"He's hanging in there," Zack said. "I talked with a buddy of mine, Striker Rheas, at Iniquus in D.C. I needed some of his hot shot hacking equipment to figure out your threats. The IP address that sent you those texts belongs to a Custis Scarborough."

"I *knew* it."

"I have a home address if you need it," Zack said.

"No, I'm well acquainted with Custis."

"There's more. Striker found two tracking apps. One is run by that Scarborough character. He's tracking you on his phone. Anywhere you take your phone, he can find you. And the other is more concerning because it's a ghost tracking app. It takes specialty equipment to find it embedded in your codes. Striker traced the connection to a burner phone."

"How did the apps get on there?"

"Have you ever put your phone down while you were out in public?"

Kate's mind went immediately to the scene of Senator Orly's heart attack. Custis had been there, and she had thrown the phone on the ground while she was trying to help the senator. She remembered finding her phone later when she was looking for evidence. "I'm sure I have."

"This is why Ryan's so paranoid about cell phones. It's easy enough to do. Striker said the second one's configurations are professional. He also said a true professional would have redundancy. Do you always carry the same purse with you?"

Kate eyed her black hobo bag. "Yes, I only brought the one with me."

"Okay, I need you to empty the bag onto a solid surface and look for anything you didn't put in there, a pen, a lighter, anything odd..."

She turned her bag upside down on her bed and spread the contents out with her hand. "How about a lipstick?" Kate pulled off the top of the golden tube and corkscrewed the red lipstick up. Definitely not a color she would wear.

"Bingo. See if you can take it apart. Are there any electrical components?"

Kate fiddled with the case. "Yes, wires, and there's a false bottom. Should I pull it all the way apart?"

"I'd hand it over to Tim and ask him what he wants to do. Striker ran the texts by his colleague, Lynx. Apparently, she's got a nose for finding trouble spots. Her feeling is that these are a juvenile attempt at scaring you or intimidating you, but she doesn't think there's intent to follow through. I'd take that with a grain of salt, though. I've never met the woman, and she's running on very little information."

"Um, okay. I don't know what to do with that."

"Striker says he's four hours away. Do you want him to come down and check on you?"

"No, thanks, Zack. I'll give this to Tim and make a plan."

"Watch your fives and twenty-fives."

ㅗㅗㅗㅗ
ㅜㅜㅜㅜ

"Katydid, I'd say you kicked a fire ant hill. I get that Custis was threatening you and keeping an eye on your movements. It seems like something he'd do. But do you really think he'd follow through by hurting you?"

"Eight people are dead, Tim. Do I want to be number nine? Not so much."

"And you think Custis killed everyone? Why? How?"

"I believe he and Doris had a plan. He has the motive – Scarborough Mining- and she had the means and the opportunity, even *if* she's your kin."

"I'm not as worried about the texts, which are pretty childish. I am concerned about this unknown person, putting trackers on your phone and in your purse. That your data is going to a burner phone tells me that someone with some skills is involved here. If this has something to do with the uranium, and they think you're getting in the way of their success, you could be in danger. We're talking about billions of dollars in revenue if the bill passes through legislation."

Kate sat at the edge of her seat, her knees pressed tightly together, her coffee forgotten in her hand.

"But if this were clearly an anti-uranium killing spree, Pemberly wouldn't have been caught up in it," Tim said.

"Unless they're trying to muddle the case. Can you think of any other connections between Wayne, Orly, Uncle Owen, and Pemberly? The killer probably drowned Cal so he couldn't tell us what he knew, and the kids were probably mistakes. Clever, too. We could have labeled every single one of their deaths accidental or inevitable."

"I probably would have, to be honest," Tim said.

"So what's the plan?"

"That depends largely on you."

⊣∪∪∟
⊤∩∩⊢

"Thanks for letting me tag along, Omid. I appreciate your letting me pick your brain about the medical questions I have. I want this case wrapped up before anyone else gets hurt." Kate spread her arms wide and tilted her head back to take in a lungful of air. "The air feels so perfect after that thundershower. Mmm, it smells like pine and rain drops."

Omid chuckled as he pulled a backpack from his trunk. "Whenever it got too hot in the city, my family would drive to the mountains. I equate walks in the woods with a calm spirit." He handed her a can of tick spray. "It's always nice to have company to share the inevitable discoveries, and I'm happy to help, if I can."

After handing the can back to Omid, Kate pulled her phone from her pocket, checked that it was fully charged and on, and that this far away from town she had enough bars. She stooped and double-tied her bootlaces. The roar of an engine made her pop back up.

Custis Scarborough jumped down from the cab of his Ram pickup, shotgun in hand. Mrs. Simpson climbed out and cowered behind the fender.

"You sonofabitch." Custis' shotgun pointed at Omid, who dropped his sack and reached his hands out to the sides, palms exposed.

Kate put her fists on her hips. "Custis Scarborough, have you been drinking? Give your gun to Mrs. Simpson and let her drive you home." Kate was surprised to hear her schoolteacher voice. She felt anything but authoritative and in control.

"Shit no, I ain't climbing back in my cab. I've got a varmint to shoot."

Mrs. Simpson put a hand on top of her head. "Custis, please, Cal wouldn't have wanted this."

"Cal," Custis said, looking at Omid. "Did you know he was my friend? Yup. Since we first went to Bible camp together. And now he's dead. Everyone would think he got drunk and passed out too close to the water. Who drowns in three inches of water? The problem with that picture is that Cal is a three-beer guy. In my whole life, even when we were teens, he never had more than three beers. You?" He glanced briefly at Cal's wife. "You ever seen him drink more than that?" Tight lipped, Brenda Simpson shook her head.

Omid took a step backward.

"Uh uh uh. I've been huntin' since I could walk," Custis said. "There ain't no way I'd miss a shot, no matter what you did. You step right up here. Get on your knees. Spread your legs wide. Now hands laced on your head."

Omid followed Custis' directives.

"As soon as I heard all them beers got him drunk, I knew someone killed him. Normally, the coroner would say accidental death. I imagine he wouldn't even check blood alcohol levels or see if someone poisoned him with some medications, huh, Doc?" Custis pointed the gun at Kate. "What about you? Did you chalk this up to an accident?"

"I thought someone slipped him a roofie and pushed him in the water to drown."

"You know why someone might want to do that? Huh, Ms. Boston Smarty Pants?" Custis demanded.

Kate could feel her hands and feet vibrate as blood rushed to her limbs, ready to help her vault to safety. Her heart pounded hard as Custis' words echoed in her ear. A shotgun at this distance would devastate both her and Omid. Her brain worked to figure out how to calm Custis and get him back in his truck.

Custis focused his aim back on Omid Javarti.

"You knew Kate was going to figure all this out, didn't you? She's smart, she is. The killer had to be someone who could access medical records. It had to be someone who could get hold of the wrong, or I guess in his mind, the right medicines. A string of bad luck. Eight people dead. Four of them kids." Custis spat on the ground. "They all lie on your head and look at you. Cool as a cucumber. Not a remorseful bone in your body."

Kate glanced down at Omid; her mouth had gone dry. "You're accusing Dr. Javarti? Why would he kill anyone?"

"Kate," Custis shouted, "shut up! Use your science. What kind of person does something like that? Kills eight people?"

Kate licked at her lips. "A psychopath, or maybe a sociopath would."

Custis glared at her. "Dr. Javarti is neither. I had to learn a lot about psychos with my shrink in juvie, because apparently psychopaths and serial killers like to start fires in their youths."

Custis scowled at Omid. "I bet you my dog Tobby, who is the one I love most in this world, that Kate had me pegged for the murderer. I'm sure she was trying to put me back behind bars. Right, Kate?" Custis turned angry eyes on her. "Psych 101? Psychopaths start off as arsonists. Only I was less an arsonist than an idiot who couldn't figure out how a prank could go so damned wrong. I didn't mean to burn down the building and hurt those families. But there's no way I could hurt Cal, or anyone else for that matter." Custis nodded his head toward Omid. "Except you, of course. I plan to shoot you. So, smarty pants, who else would do it?"

Kate's mind went blank. *What should I say? What should I do?* They all stood there, waiting for her to come up with some kind of answer. "Um, someone with a vengeance."

"Nope. It's not that, either. He's got no gripe with any of us here."

Kate hated this game. The sun beat on her head. Squinting past the glare, Kate tried again. "People will kill serially for a cause they've taken as an oath, like soldiers."

"Bingo. That's it, isn't it, Doc? You're a college professor in Iran, and got a sudden hankerin' to go fishing? So you packed your bag and came to Scarborough, Virginia, with three stop lights and an ice cream shop." Custis stalled and stared into the woods to their right. "I bet it's killed you, hanging out with all us hicks. I bet you were thrilled to have someone from Boston show up. Only you weren't counting on that someone turning out to be an insipid know-it-all. She figured out OC tablets are a scarcity. She figured out the Nitro was sugar."

Kate was astonished that Custis knew all this.

Custis moved his attention to the tree line behind her. Goose bumps prickled Kate's flesh.

"Small towns have trouble keeping their secrets," Custis murmured.

Kate looked over at Brenda Simpson. Brenda had her gaze fastened over Omid's head.

"Smarty pants thinks she knows why they died," Custis said. "She thinks it's all about the upcoming vote on mining. That's my motive for killing everyone. Let's see how that works out. Let's tick them off. Tredegar Orly was a big one. No one would thwart him in the legislature. Oh look, he's no longer an issue. And then there was Wayne Brody. He was leading the opposition on the environmental front. He was a real crusader for the river. Wasn't he? And what do we know about groups and their leaders?"

He waited expectantly, but no one answered.

"Nothing to say? Well, America knows what to do. Look at Al Qaeda. Take out the leaders and the rest run around like headless chickens, not knowing what to do next. That's pretty much true for any group dynamic. Last minute like this, there's no time to rally the troops. The environmentalists are floundering. So check them off the list. Now there's Pemberly. Why, oh why, take out Pemberly? She was on uranium's side. Maybe I was trying to throw the cops off the scent? Could be. Damn sure if the legislature got wind that people were getting killed off to make the vote go through, they couldn't very well vote 'yes,' now could they?"

Kate looked at Brenda Simpson. She nodded her head, then climbed in the cab, shut and locked the door.

Custis kept talking. "I'll tell you why. Pemberly was not only expendable; she was strategic. She didn't want to sell her investment in SM to American Mine Works. She wanted to hold on and go for the mountains of cash rather than take the moolah hill and be happy. Her hubby, on the other hand, thought differently, now didn't he? If Pemberly were dead, hubby would sell their SM investment to American Mine Works as quick as he could get his signature on the paperwork. My understanding is that he has power-of-attorney now that she's batshit crazy and locked up in a loony bin. Maybe Jason was the mastermind behind all of these deaths. He wanted the legislation to go through, but if it were looking bad, then he could just sign the American Mine Works' papers. Either way, he never had to lift a finger for the rest of his life. He's cousins with Doris Arthur. He had access to the pharmacy."

Custis took in a deep breath and shook his head on the exhale. "Yeah, but Jason's also an idiot. Which leads us to here and now. Why am I holding a shotgun on Dr. Omid Javarti?"

Kate tasted the tang of blood from where she'd chewed a small hole in her lip.

"We all know from reading the Scarborough Sun this morning that American Mine Works is an offshore company that no one has ever heard of before. And I can tell you for certain, seeings how it was in my best interest to find out, that the business is buried beneath so many layers of secrecy, we can't figure out who owns it. Could it be that Iran might be interested in having their finger in the uranium pie? There's a stretch of the imagination." Custis laughed without mirth.

Kate's stomach heaved like she was plummeting from a very high roller coaster.

"Now everyone knows I've got no love for that woman." Custis briefly directed the shotgun at Kate. "Quite frankly, I'd like to see her suffer some. But I'll be damned if I'm going to let some Iranian come to my town, and kill my people, and let her get caught in your net."

Kate desperately wanted to sit down. Her knees shook. Fear and heat made her dizzy. She had never had a gun aimed at her before.

Custis refocused on Omid. "That's why you're here with her tonight, ain't it? You planned for her to have a little accident. Can't drown her. You already did that to poor Cal." Custis shook his head. "He was desperate. Someone's funding you big time, Doc. And you snared Cal. He could suddenly give his family what he always wanted to give them. And they didn't go homeless. Imagine the pull a man felt with a daughter in desperate straits, huh?"

Custis took a step forward. Kate could see disdain curling the skin by his nose.

His voice took on an eerie softness. "So here you are with Kate. You can't drown her like Cal. You can't mis-medicate her like the others. She wouldn't dare take a prescription filled in Scarborough." He canted his head. "How did you kill Tredegar and Ow-Owen once they were in your care? I'm thinking air in their IV lines. Am I right? Something undetectable so it would never get traced back to you. And now you have to kill again, and this has to be a good one. Kate, go check his bag over there."

Curious, Kate did as she was asked. There was silence while she rifled through Omid's things. She sat back on her heels, staring incredulously at a vial of insulin and hypodermic needles.

"What you got there, Kate?" Custis called.

"This would do it," Kate held up the vial. "We studied the Kenneth Barlow case where he injected his wife's buttocks with insulin, and she died. Modern tests would easily show an excess of insulin in the tissue."

Everyone stood silent, watching her studying the vial dangling in her fingers, mind far away.

"It's so hot," Kate said. "What if I went for a hike? Omid gave me the shot, and then called the police to say I went missing, and he couldn't find me. If he started the search off in the wrong location…we're expecting hundred degree temperatures for the next three days. My body would be too decomposed for them to find insulin."

She stood, moving closer to Custis, her eyes fixed on Omid. "If I were in a hypoglycemic coma, you could crack my head down on a rock to make it look like I fell."

Custis took a step forward. The barrel of the gun hung a mere foot from Omid's head. "You sonofabitch, I'm gonna tell you something certain. You know, just like I know, just like everyone in the whole blessed town knows, Tim and Kate were a thing. And they still care for each other. That spark never quite left his eye. And if Tim thought someone had hurt Kate? Shoot, he'd follow that sonofabitch into the bowels of Hell to make things right. Wouldn't you, Tim?"

Kate spun around to see Tim and four other officers step from behind the trees. Tim cuffed Omid and pulled him to his feet.

"You can't arrest me on the ranting of that man. He's insane," Omid scoffed.

"Oh, but I can arrest you on murder charges," Tim said. "When Cal plotted with you about slipping the wrong meds into the pharmacy bags, he videotaped the whole thing. He knew his chances of surviving weren't spectacular. He wanted to make sure that if he got caught, he didn't go down alone. And if he were killed, that his family would know the truth. I have all the evidence I need up at the station. Mrs. Simpson found the DVD and a note in their safety deposit box when she went to get Cal's will for their lawyer, who happens to be Custis Scarborough."

Tim focused on Kate. "You okay, Katydid?"

"About damned time you showed up." She reached under her shirt and pulled at the wires taped to her belly. "Guess we don't need this after all."

Tim grinned. "Wasn't sure what to make of things when Custis beat us to the punch."

Kate looked at Tim, then at Custis. "He did that in spades. Thank you, Custis, for trying to save my life. You figured out the mystery."

"Weren't just me." He pointed his finger around the circle. "Small towns stand tight."

Kate moved closer to Custis. "They do indeed."

THE END

Did you have fun reading MINE? It was such an interesting story for me to write. I hope you'll recommend my book to your friends who might enjoy this story, too. The best way for you to share your honest review of my work, is to post a quick few sentences on Amazon and Goodreads. Tell people what you liked about it, then give this book some stars. Please do that. Your efforts will be much appreciated – and I won't forget your help.

Want to be the first to know about upcoming releases?
Fiona Quinn's Mailing List. - http://goo.gl/97x0QX

This spring, I am thrilled to bring you **WEAKEST LYNX**.
Serial killers, spy games, psychic links, special ops guys, and
a kick-ass heroine **Lexi Sobado** who is
Unschooled -- Unconventional - Unstoppable.
All kinds of fun!
I hope you enjoy this excerpt…

Weakest Lynx

The black BMW was coming straight at me. Heart pounding, I stomped the brake pedal flush to the floorboard. My chest slammed into the seat belt. My head snapped forward. No time to blast the horn, but the scream from my tires was deafening. The BMW idiot threw me a nonchalant wave – his right hand off the wheel, with his left hand pressed to his ear still chatting on his cell phone. Diplomatic license plates. *Figures.*

Yeah, I didn't really need an extra shot of adrenaline, like a caffeine I.V. running straight to an artery. I was already amped. My breath hissed between my teeth, relieving some of my tension as I sent a quick glance down to my purse. A corner of a cream-colored envelope jutted out.

Focus, Lexi. Follow the plan. Give the letter to Dave and leave. Let him work this out.

The near miss with the BMW guy probably wasn't all his fault. I couldn't remember the last ten minutes of drive time. Pressing down on the gas, I veered my Camry back into the noonday gridlock weaving past the graffiti-ed storefronts of D.C.

Inching through the bumper-to-bumper traffic, I focused on my review mirror as a bike messenger laced between the moving cars on his suicide mission to get the parcel in his bag to the right guy at the right time. Once he handed over his package, he'd be done. Lucky him. I knew that handing over my letter to Dave was going to be just the beginning.

When I finally parked in front of Dave Murphy's mid-century brick row house, I sat for a minute, not quite ready to go inside. I'd pushed this whole mess to the back burner, but after last night's nightmare... Well, better to get a professional opinion from someone who'd been handling crackpots for a while. Dealing with this letter and the nut case who wrote the darn thing required something beyond the heebie-jeebies, and Criminal Psych 101 textbook that I brought to the table.

Overall, this has been a pretty suckish week, I glanced down at my hands. The tremor in them sent the afternoon sunlight dancing off my brand new engagement and wedding rings. I felt like an imposter wearing them - like a little girl dressed up in her mother's clothes. *I'm too young to be dealing with all of this crap*, I thought as I shoved my keys into my purse. I pulled my long blond hair into a quick ponytail. I couldn't let another minute pass by. Taking a deep breath, I stepped out into the February cold and cast an anxious glance up and down the street.

When I ran up the stairs and banged on Dave's front door the screen squeaked open almost immediately, as if he'd been standing there, waiting for my knock.

"Hey, Baby Girl," he said, stepping out of the way. "Come on in."

"Thanks. Glad I found you at home." I walked in and plopped down on the blue gingham couch. It had been here since I could remember. The fabric was threadbare and juice stained, probably by his twins. On a cop's salary, fine furnishings ranked low in priority. Right now – edgy and confused – I appreciated the comfort of familiarity.

Dave shifted into detective mode – hands on hips, eyes scanning me. "Long time, no see."

"Where are Cathy and the kids?" I asked.

"They've got dentist appointments. Did you come to tell us your news?" He pointed at my left hand and settled at the other end of the couch, swiveling so we were face to face.

"Uhm, no." I twisted my rings, suddenly feeling drained and bereft. What I wouldn't give to have Angel here. The corners of my mouth tugged down. I willed myself to stay focused on the reason for the visit. My immediate safety had to take priority over self-pity.

Dave raised a questioning brow, waiting for me to continue.

"I got married Wednesday. I'm Lexi Sobado, now." My voice hitched and tears pressed against my lids. I lowered my lashes so Dave wouldn't see. But I knew his eyes had locked onto mine.

"Married? At your age? No introduction? No wedding invitation? Why isn't he here with you now?" Dave angled his head to the side and crossed his arms over his slight paunch. "I'd like to meet the guy." He all but snarled.

Dave must think I'd come here because my husband screwed things up already. I pulled the pillow from behind my back and hugged it to me like a shield. "I'm sorry. I should have let you and Cathy know what was going on – I was caught up, and I just..." I stopped to clear my throat. "Angel and I got married at the courthouse and no one came with us. Not even Abuela Rosa."

"Angel Sobado. He's kin to Rosa?"

I nodded. "Angel is her great-nephew. I couldn't bring him with me today because he deployed to the Middle East Thursday. That's why everything happened so fast. He was leaving." The last word stuck in my throat and choked me.

Dave leaned forward to rest his elbows on his knees. Lacing his fingers, he tapped his thumbs together. "Huh. Well, that's a helluva short honeymoon, Lexi. Married on Wednesday and gone by Thursday." Dave's tone had dropped an octave and gained a fringe of concern.

His compassion gave me permission to break down. But those Angel-emotions were mine. Private. Right now, I needed to hold myself in check long enough to get through my mission. I chewed my lower lip, and shifted my feet back and forth, glaring at my purse.

"Might even explain the expression on your face," Dave said, narrowing his eyes. He slouched against the arm of the over-stuffed couch and waited me out. When I couldn't stall any longer, I reached a hesitant hand into my bag, pulled out a plastic Zip-loc holding the envelop, and held it up for Dave.

"The expression is because of this," I said.

Dave took the bag. After a brief glance, he laid the vile thing on his coffee table and hefted himself to his feet. Over at his desk, he pulled on a pair of latex gloves, then carefully removed the letter.

Dearest India Alexis,

O my Luve's like the melodie
That's sweetly play'd in tune!
As fair thou art, my bonnie lass,
So deep in love am I:
And I will love thee still, my dear,
Till a' your bones are white and dry:
Till a' your veins gang dry, my dear,

And your skin melt with the sun;

I will luve thee until your heart is still my dear

When the sands of your life shall no more run.

And fare thee weel, my only Luve,

And fare thee weel a while!

And I will come again, my Luve, so I can watch you die.

Dave read the words aloud then stared at me hard; his brows pulled in so tight the skin on his forehead accordioned. "What the…"

"Someone slid the poem under my door, and it's scaring the bejeezus out of me." I gripped the pillow tighter.

Dave peered over the top of his reading glasses. "Last night? This morning?"

"Wednesday morning." I braced when I said it, knowing it would tick Dave off that I waited to bring the letter to him. Ever since my dad died, his buddies had stepped in and tried to take over the fathering job, even though I'd be turning twenty in a few days.

True to my expectations, Dave was red-faced and bellowing. "*Wednesday?* You waited two whole days to tell me you've gotten a friggin death threat?"

Yup, this was exactly the response Dad would have given me.

Dave jumped up, pacing across the room. Obviously, he didn't think this was someone's idea of a joke. Fear tightened my chest at this confirmation. I had hoped he'd say, "No worries – someone is having fun pranking you," and then I could go on about my life without the major case of heebie-jeebies that tingled my skin and made me want to run and hide.

"It was our wedding day." I modulated my voice to sound soft and reasonable. "I only had a few short hours before Angel had to take off. So yeah, I decided to focus on us instead of this." I motioned towards the paper in his hand.

Dave took in a deep breath, making his nostrils flare. "Okay." I could almost see his brain shifting gears. "When you first picked up the letter, did you get any vibes?"

I considered him carefully. "You mean... ESP-wise?" He nodded stiffly, his eyes hard on me.

Vibes. That wasn't the word I would have chosen to explain my sensations. "I didn't hear anything. It was as if an oily substance oozed over me. I vomited." I tucked my nose into the soft cloth of the pillow and breathed in the scent of cinnamon fabric freshener. My voice dropped to a whisper. "It felt like evil and craziness, and I can still smell the stench." A shiver raced down my spine.

Dave's lips sealed tightly; he was probably trying to hold back a litany of expletives. Finally, he asked, "That's all?"

"So far."

"Did any of your neighbors notice anyone unusual lurking around? Did you check with management and run through the security tapes?"

"Dave, didn't you hear? My apartment building burned to the ground three weeks ago. I assumed you knew. It was on the news…"

Dave's eyebrows shot straight up.

"I've been living in a motel the Red Cross rented out for all the families from my old apartment building. But to answer your question, no, nobody saw anything, and there were no cameras trained on my motel corridor." I bit at my lips to keep them from trembling. I was used to holding my emotions in check, presenting a sweet exterior, but right now I was filled to over-flowing, and my mask kept slipping out of place.

"Shit, I had no idea." Dave ran a hand over his face. "Jeezis, Lexi. I'm letting your parents down. Apartment burned, married, husband gone, and now a stalker… Do you think that about covers all of your surprises for me today?"

I slit my eyes and paused for a beat. "Yeah, Dave, I think that's it for today." Okay, even if he was like family, the way Dave was talking still pissed me off. I was frightened. I wanted a hug and his reassurance. What I was getting was… Dave's brand of love. He

146

wouldn't be this red-faced and agitated if he wasn't worried about me. Tears prickled behind my eyelids, blurring my vision.

"Hey, now. Stop. We'll get to the bottom of this. Did you already let Spyder McGraw know what's going on?"

I wiped my nose with the back of my wrist. "Spyder's still off-grid. I have no idea when he'll get home."

"Were you assigned a different partner while he's gone?"

"No, sir. I only ever worked for Spyder – he sort of wanted to keep me a secret." I still couldn't believe Mom had sat Dave down and told him all about my apprenticeship with Spyder McGraw. Under Spyder's tutelage, I was following my dream of becoming an Intelligence Officer, learning to out-think and out-maneuver the bad guys trying to hurt American interests. Only four people – Spyder, the Millers, and Dave – knew that side of me. I would prefer Dave didn't know.

"Still, did you consider bringing this to Spyder's commander? Iniquus would probably give him a heads up. Get a message to him."

"Iniquus is my last resort. Sure, Spyder told me to talk to them if I ever found myself in trouble." I sucked in a deep breath of air. "Bottom line? He never wanted them to know I worked for him, well, for them... Safety in anonymity and all that." My fingers kneaded the stuffing in the pillow. "Besides, I guess I was hoping this would all just go away."

Dave's eyes were hard and unblinking. "You know better. Once some psycho's caught you on his radar, you're stuck there until someone wins."

"So I need to make sure it's me who wins." I moved the pillow to the side and rubbed my palms on my thighs to dry them.

"Exactly right." He considered me for a minute. "You've kept up with your martial arts training?"

"I have a sparring partner who's pretty good. We rent time at a Do Jang twice a week."

I focused up where the ceiling and the wall made a shadowed crease while Dave read over the poem again. He put the letter and envelope back in the Zip-loc and placed it on his mantle.

Pulling off his gloves with a snap, he looked down at them. "Jeez, I hate these things. They give me a rash. Look, I'm going to take this down to the station and open a file. If you get anything else, I want you to bring it to me right away. Understood?"

"Yes, sir."

"This is the only poem, letter, communication of any kind you've gotten?"

I nodded. For the first time since I came into Dave's house, I became aware of sounds other than our conversation and the thrumming of blood behind my eardrums. A football game played on TV. I glanced over as the announcer yelled some gibberish about a first down, then back at Dave. "You must have taken graveyard shift last night," I said.

He picked up a remote, zapped off the TV, and sent me a raised eyebrow.

"It doesn't take a psychic. You look like an unmade bed."

Dave ran a hand over his dark hair, thick on the sides, sparse on top. He hadn't used a comb today or bothered to shave. He was hanging-out-at-home comfy in jeans, and beat-to-hell tennis shoes. It looked like the only thing I was interrupting was the game re-run.

"Double homicide. Turned into a long night up to my ankles in sewage."

"Yum." I tried on a smile, but it was plastic and contrived.

Dave narrowed his eyes. "We need to move you. Pronto. It's priority one. You need to be someplace secure where I can keep better tabs on you."

"I've been looking since the fire, but I haven't found anything."

"Would you consider buying?" he asked.

"Yes – I want a low-cost fixer-upper I can work on to help me get through this year without Angel. Diversion, and all that." I waggled my hand in the air.

"How about here, in my neighborhood? I could keep a better eye on you – and you won't be showing up at my door with a suitcase full of surprises."

I grimaced and followed Dave into the hallway. He grabbed his coat from the closet and shrugged it on. "I'm taking you over to meet my neighbor. She has the other half of her duplex on the market." He looked over his shoulder at me. "You shouldn't be running around without a jacket." He handed me an oversized wool parka that smelled like raking leaves. He kicked a Tonka truck out of the way to shut the door.

On the front porch, I slid into the shadows and took in the length of the road. No cars, no barking dogs, everything quiet. Dave glanced back. "Coast is clear."

Screened by Dave's broad back, I started across the street. Down the road, a car motor revved. I reached under my shirt and pulled out my gun.

End of excerpt

To read more go to:

http://www.fionaquinnbooks.com/#!WeakestLynx/c1aa3

Acknowledgements

My husband, Todd, is always my first thought when I am expressing gratitude. He makes it possible for me to write, which is the thing I love most to do. Todd had a big hand in developing this story. I truly appreciate all the ways he has helped me big and small, with constancy and love.

I also want to thank my kid #4. She lies on the floor and listens to me read to her. Somehow, her listening is the magic I need to find the mistakes in my writing – and it doesn't hurt that she has an awesome little-miss-know-it-all bag handy from which she pulls obscure facts that help me get the details right – I can thank her for not writing that Aunt Emma's new cat was a male calico in this story.

A HUGE thank you to B. Boswell for help with medical information and regional dialect.

My appreciation to Dr. Scott Silverii. Scott introduced me to the Unlucky Seven project. I had never written a novella length piece before and had not tried my hand at a small town murder mystery. I had so much fun working on this project as I joined forces with six other writers to put together the Unlucky Seven Collection, where this novel began its journey. Thank you to Jamie Lee Scott for her tireless work making Unlucky Seven a go; to Teresa Watson, who saw that I was flailing in the brackish waters where my English-English and America-English spelling collided (as I was cross working on this project and a project with author John Dolan, CHAOS IS COME AGAIN written in English-English). She threw me a lifeline.

Thank you also to the other writers, Diane Capri, Tawny Stokes, and Hildie McQueen from whom I learned a ton and with whom I laughed even more.

But mostly – thank YOU for reading my work, sharing your thoughts, and being wonderful.

About the Author

Canadian born, I am now rooted in the Old Dominion outside of D.C. with my husband and four children. I homeschool, pop chocolates, devour books, and tap continuously on my laptop. For more about me, visit my bio page at:

http://www.FionaQuinnBooks.com

Please stay in touch:

My newsletter: http://goo.gl/97x0QX

https://www.twitter.com/FionaQuinnBooks

https://www.facebook.com

Made in the USA
Monee, IL
29 June 2020